Derry
Air

by Garth Wallace

Published by:
Happy Landings

Other books by Garth Wallace:

Fly Yellow Side Up
Pie In The Sky
Blue Collar Pilots
Don't Call Me a Legend

Canadian Catalogue Data:

Derry Air
fiction, aviation, humour

Written by:
Wallace, Garth 1946 -

ISBN 0-969-7322-4-4

C813'.54

Editing:
Liz Wallace
Sari Funston

Cover Art:
Francois Bougie

Typesetting and proofreading:
Ohlmann Editorial and Design

Written, typeset, printed and bound in Canada

Published by:
Happy Landings
RR #4
Merrickville, Ontario
K0G 1N0
Tel.: 613-269-2552
E-mail: orders@happylanding.com

Contact the author: garth@happylanding.com

Contents

Introduction

Blame it on the mirth generated by the crazy name or the thin air. Whatever it was, Derry Air changed people. Ordinary customers and staff were transformed when they walked through those flying school doors. Marathon Melville, Barnacle Bill and Beautiful Bob were proof. So were Huey, Duey and Louey. I met and worked with the world's most entertaining characters at Derry Air.

My initial plan had been to teach there long enough to grab an Instrument Rating, build twin-engine flying time, bag a check-out in a high-performance airplane and escape to the airlines, but it changed me too. I arrived believing Derry Air was a stepping stone to a high-priced airline job. I left knowing that the important things in life were not money, position or career but what you're doing and who you're doing it with. As you read this book you will be sharing good times with funny people. In life, you could do a lot worse.

Garth Wallace
Merrickville, Ontario
September, 1997

Acknowledgment

Derry Air is fiction. Any resemblance to actual people and events is a coincidence. There is, however, an existing air service called Derry Air. It's a bush flying operation attached to Gogama Lodge in Gogama, Ontario, Canada. None of the stories in this book came from the real Derry Air. The author is grateful to the owners of that air service for having a great sense of humor and for granting permission to use the name for this book.

If you like to laugh, read this book. If you like to hunt and fish in the bush, call Gogama Lodge, Tel.: 705-894-2770.

Chapter One

For better or worse

Irving Mingy was doing the impossible. He was making money in aviation. Mingy owned and managed a flying school and charter operation at the airport in the city of Derry. The secrets of his success included a hands-on knowledge of the flying business and a vicious cheapness that would have embarrassed Robbie Burns.

I didn't know Mingy or his ways but I did know his company operated twin-engine aircraft. An instructor friend who flew there told me that Mingy's pilots could work their way into the charter department and then get hired by an airline. This was important to me. I was instructing at a small town flying school. I had reached the stage in my career where I realized there must be more to aviation than flying for long underpaid days in drafty training airplanes with student pilots trying to kill me.

While my customers practised their flying maneuvers, I dreamed about flying for the airline industry: a warm cockpit, sophisticated equipment, consecutive days off, in-flight coffee service and a six-figure income. To qualify, I needed an Instrument Rating and experience flying multi-engine aircraft. Both were available at Mingy's operation at the Derry Airport.

That's why I was standing outside Mingy's office, staring at him. I couldn't help staring. The man looked like an aging welterweight boxer with a losing record.

"Come in," he said. "Leave the door open." His tone matched a sour expression on his badly scarred face.

The office was small and bare. He was sitting on the only chair.

"Why do you want to work here?" he asked straight out. There was no, "How do you do?" or "Pleased to meet you." Not this man.

Mingy was glaring at me like a high school vice-principal who could read thoughts and spot lies miles away. I didn't think I could tell him the truth. I couldn't say that I wanted to scoop an Instrument Rating from his school, build some twin-engine time, bag a checkout on the 10-passenger Piper Navajo from his charter department and then skip to the airlines.

"As an experienced Class II flying instructor," I said, crossing my fingers behind my back, "I decided joining an operation like yours would give me the opportunity to earn more revenue. The small school where I work closes at six. I'm just warmed up after four or five hours flying and it's time to go home."

Mingy clenched his teeth and flexed his facial scars. "That's bull," he said. He was right. "If you want to work here, get some multi-engine time and then move on, that's fine with me. But if you want to stand around and spin tales, go somewhere else."
I was no match for Mingy.

"I'll work," I said.

"Same terms as everyone else," he replied. "Twelve dollars per revenue hour, payable at the end of the following month."

I did a quick mental calculation: five revenue hours per good day and 200 "good days" a year optimistically added up to $12,000. It wasn't bad; about the same as I was already making and only $2,000 below the poverty line. Mingy was charging $32 an hour for his instructors' time, but he would have to pay benefits out of that.

"All my pilots work on contract," he continued. "Set up your own company and bill me for services rendered, just like a plumber. That way you look after your own benefits and insurance. It saves me a lot of paperwork."

It saved him a lot of money too. With holiday pay and minimum benefits, the $12 an hour would have been $17. Now it would be more like $8. The dream of using Derry Air to vault into the airlines was fading. I might starve to death before accumulating the experience to get hired. No wonder airline copilots were always skinnier than the captains.

"If you want to train on the school Twin Comanche, it's available at a staff rate of $50 an hour."

Now the man was talking my language. I would need about 20 hours for a Multi-engine Instrument Rating and Mingy had just saved me $1,000.

"Between midnight and six in the morning," he added.

"Oh thanks a lot, tightwad," I said, but only in my mind. Next I expected him to tell me I'd have to pay to park my car. I was close.

"Tell Angel that you're going to start and give her $20 for the first month's coffee fund."

That was it. I finally spoke up. "I don't drink coffee," I protested weakly. "And I have to give my employer notice."

"The coffee is for the customers. I already spoke to John Torrance," Mingy said.

I fought to keep my jaw from dropping to the floor. I hadn't mentioned to my present boss anything about leaving his Pie In The Sky flying school. Mingy was way ahead of me.

"He said you are a good instructor. I hope you prove him right. Leave the door open on the way out."

He looked down at the ledger on his desk indicating the interview was over. I could tell him to go jump in the lake or I could thank him and leave.

"I'll do my best, sir," I said.

I turned and walked out the door. I felt numb. Mingy's "terms" took the edge off the idea of changing jobs. I decided that I could tell the receptionist that I would start a week Monday. That would give me time to think about it and maybe change my mind. Then my only problem would be that I didn't have $20 for the coffee fund.

Angel was squatting on a stool behind the flight desk. She looked like one of those fat, blubbery characters from a bar in a Star Wars movie. I felt sorry for the stool. The receptionist was wearing a tent dress from the Bargain Barn. It was topped with a face that could have been used for stamping cheese. As I approached the flight desk in front of her, I hoped a kindly soul might be buried under all the warts and unruly hair.

I fixed a smile on my face and said, "Hi. Irving asked me to tell you when I'm going to start instructing here."

"The man's name is Mister Mingy," she said flatly.

I had wakened a monster. "Sorry, M- Mi- Ms-"

"Angel, you call me Angel. You ask me when you can start and I give you a date."

Apparently Mr. Mingy owned the operation, but Angel ran it.

"You got the twenty bucks?" she asked.

"No," I replied.

"Bring it with you next time. When do you want to start?"

I was still reeling from her initial outburst, but I realized Angel was softening already. "I was hoping to start a week Monday." I tried to sound humble.

"Bad day," she said. "Two airplanes are booked off for maintenance and the instructors will be fighting over what's left.

9

Start Tuesday, I should be able to line up some students for you then."

"Okay, thank you."

Before I turned to go, Angel leaned toward me and said in a lowered voice, "The coffee money is just Mr. Mingy's funny way of making you part of the team. Bring it on Tuesday and he won't ask for it again."

"Thanks for the tip," I said, and departed shaking my head.

This was a different kind of place. I wasn't sure if I wanted to work there or not, but I still had a week to either change my mind or learn to drink coffee.

Outside, a Piper Navajo was parked on the ramp. Three young linemen were cleaning the windshield and the engine cowlings on the wings. I walked toward it. The Navajo was a big airplane compared to what I had been flying. The stairs in the lower half of the rear door hung down. I asked the nearest lineman if I could look inside.

"Sure," he said.

I climbed the steps and looked forward. The passenger seats on either side of the centre aisle were leather. I drank in their rich smell as I walked bent over to the cockpit and looked between the two pilot seats. I was seeing more equipment than I had before. My strong need for a change was reawakened. I could enjoy flying an airplane like this.

I climbed out of the airplane. Henry Rains, my instructor friend who worked there, was across the ramp supervising a student's walkaround inspection on a Piper Twin Comanche. I waved. He smiled and waved back.

I looked at the modern flight lounge built onto the runway side of the big, old World War II hangar. The sign over the door read, "Welcome to Derry Air".

I had made up my mind. It was time to move on and up. I was going to work for a company called Derry Air, for better or worse.

Chapter Two

Melville forever

I went home to the town of Pie and told my wife that I had landed the job. Susan had been working with me as the receptionist at the Pie In The Sky flying school.

She belted out a big, "Yahoo!"

"No more learning the dumb pilot lingo on the office radio!" she whooped. "No more log books. No more Hector's dirty looks."

Susan's main interest was horses. I was aware that working for a pilot husband had been getting to her, but now I knew how much. Taking the job at Derry was a good idea.

Pie was a two-hour drive away from my new job. We planned to move. That evening we were discussing where we would stay until we found a place of our own, when Henry Rains phoned.

"Did you get the job?" he asked enthusiastically.

"I sure did. Thanks for your help."

"When do you start and where are you going to live?"

"A week Tuesday and we don't know."

"Stay here until you find a place. We'd love to have you."

The "we" was Henry, his wife, Leanne and their two kids, Vicious and Greedy. Those were my names for them. Leanne was nice but she was an earth-mother type with a laisser-faire approach to raising her children. Victor and Gretchen had the run of the house and god help anyone in their way.

I thanked Henry for the offer and told him we'd let them know.

"It might not be bad for a few days," I said to Susan.

She wrinkled her nose. "I get along fine with Leanne, but I'm afraid of the mortal combat that might break out between you and the kids."

"You're right but Henry would be offended if we rented a motel room. Besides, we can't afford it."

"Now you're right."

We bit the bullet and moved into the Rain's guest room in the basement. We avoided the kids as much as possible. Susan and our German Shepherd dog, Lady, spent the days touring Derry in our Volkswagen Beetle looking for a house. I went to work with Henry.

On my first day, we left home early so I could meet some of the staff. We arrived to find the receptionist squatting on the same stool in the same tent dress as the week before. Angel took my $20 coffee money and showed me the schedule. I couldn't believe it. I was booked to fly most of the day. New instructors normally build their student list slowly by phoning customer dropouts and by being available for new student introductory flying lessons.

Henry told me later that Angel never allowed an old customer list to develop. She maintained weekly contact with all the students and made sure they were booked. The result was that the school was busy and I was filling their need for another instructor.

I met Derry Air's chief flying instructor, Eric Daedalus. He had a permanent round grin and a roly-poly body to match. He seemed like the exact opposite of our sour boss, Irving Mingy.

"Henry told me that you have lots of Cherokee time," he said when we were introduced.

"Yes sir," I replied.

"Eric," he corrected. "Did he outline my philosophy on rules and regulations?"

Henry had indeed. He said that Eric had no rules or regulations. His philosophy was that the government had already over-regulated aviation and there was no need to add more.

"Yes sir, he has," I replied.

"Eric," he corrected again.

"Yes sir, Eric."

He laughed. My first impression was that working for Eric could be fun.

The rest of the time before giving my first lesson was spent with Henry going over the files of my students for the day. It soon became obvious that they were the "deadwood" cast off by the other flying staff. I started the day doing landing practise with an accountant whose coke-bottle glasses made the runway appear further away than it was. He flared out perfectly about 50 feet above the runway, every time. Then I flew with the middle-aged housewife whose husband was the only one in the world who wanted her to fly. She closed her eyes most of the time and all the time near the ground. Finally, I flew with the absent-minded dentist who lost control of the Cherokee when he tried to stick his arm out the little side window to signal a turn. By 15:30 in the afternoon, I was still alive, but I was scheduled to fly with Melville Passmore next. I didn't know what to expect but I feared the worst.

Melville looked like a Melville: short, round and farmer friendly. When we were introduced, he gave me a big grin and shook my arm like it was the handle on a water pump. Melville hooked his thumbs under his overall straps when he talked and left his tongue hanging out between sentences.

Being assigned to a new flying instructor didn't seem to bother Melville. He launched right into his life story about living with his folks on a farm near the airport. He helped his dad and saved his money for flying lessons. He loved airplanes. I listened politely while flipping through his pilot log book.

According to the log, Melville had flown 73 hours over the last nine months with eleven different instructors. After the first few entries, most of the lessons were "takeoffs and landings". He had practised in the airport circuit for over 60 hours. He had never soloed.

"I got lots of hours, don't I?" Melville said. He sounded worried about my reaction.

"Do you have your student pilot permit Melville?" I asked.

"Yup, sure do," he said, pulling out his wallet and carefully extracting a dog-eared piece of paper. He proudly unfolded it with his stubby fingers and handed it to me.

The permit was six months old. Its existence meant that Melville was physically fit to hold a pilot licence, mentally smart enough to pass a couple of air regulations tests, and had covered all the pre-solo flying lessons. It was the second last thing he needed before being sent on his own. The last was an instructor's signature. The space was blank.

"I just wanta go solo," Melville volunteered while I was trying to decide what to do with him. "If I went solo, I wouldn't care if I ever flew again."

I was beginning to sense that Melville had fallen through the cracks of the normal learn-to-fly process. Most student pilots go solo by 20 hours. The unwritten law governing instructors' sanity dictates that the few students who don't go solo by 20 hours are supposed to give up the sport. The round little farmer had already spent more money than most people do on the whole course. It wasn't right. I decided Melville had finally met the flying instructor who was going to do something for him, one way or the other.

"What are we goin' to do today?" he asked patiently.

"Melville," I said with a big gush of confidence, "today you and I are going to practise takeoffs and landings."

Repeating the same lesson sounded like a cop out, but staying in the airport circuit was the fastest way to see how badly he flew.

Melville didn't mind. He had been worried that I would find an excuse to cancel the lesson. He had seen it before.

"Which plane do we have? I'll check 'er over," he said enthusiastically.

"We're flying TVH and we'll check it over together," I replied. If this kid was as bad as his record, he wasn't going to touch the airplane without supervision.

Melville eagerly scampered around the Piper Cherokee 140 while I watched. He seemed to know what he was doing. He answered my questions about the airplane and gave me a passenger safety briefing before we started up. He was careful and slow. He listened to the automatic terminal information on the radio three times before laboriously printing the runway number on a kneepad. He called the Derry Airport Ground Control for a taxi clearance, yelling into the microphone as if he didn't trust the radio to do the amplifying for him. The controller must have recognized Melville's voice. He answered slowly. Melville, tongue out all the way, hung on his every word.

Melville taxied the airplane cautiously to the active runway and completed a pre-takeoff check. So far he was doing better than the three students I had flown with earlier.

When we were cleared to takeoff, Melville hunched over the wheel, stuck out his tongue and grinned at me from ear to ear.

"You ready?" he asked.

"Let her rip," I replied.

I poised over my set of controls hoping to catch whatever surprises Melville had in store for me. There were none. He did a good takeoff, flew a nearly perfect circuit, and did an excellent touch and go. We went around the airport three times and I never had to touch the controls or say anything.

Now the challenge was finding out why nobody would let him go solo. On Melville's next landing flareout, I shoved my control wheel forward which bounced the airplane back into the air off its nose wheel. Melville recovered perfectly. I kicked the rudder pedals on takeoff, slewing the airplane down the runway. Melville straightened us out with no problem. The little tests caused his tongue to come out further, but he had obviously played those games before. On the next landing I asked the control tower to give us an overshoot. He handled that without any difficulty.

For an hour, Melville showed me that he was basically a good pilot. The whole time we were up, there were three or four other flying school aircraft in the Derry Airport circuit. Melville just followed the Cessna ahead of us. As 17:00 approached, the airport started to get busy. A couple of airliners came on the frequency, inbound for their late afternoon pickups. Two Derry-based executive aircraft called in returning home. A few after-work training flights joined the fray.

"Wanna do a full stop this time?" Melville asked. He looked worried.

"No, let's do one more touch and go. Pretend the flaps don't work this time."

The control tower was busy. "Tango Victor Hotel, extend your downwind, you're now number five behind a Metroliner joining the base leg from the northeast. Watch for a Learjet inbound from the east."

Melville didn't reply. He flew on as if the tower was talking to someone else.

"Melville, he was talking to you," I said.

No reply. Melville flew on as if I was speaking to someone else.

When he turned toward the airport, obviously following the Cessna, I took over control and turned outbound to make room for the approaching airliner. "Melville, see this other guy? We have to follow him."

"Are we going to do a full stop now?"

"Yes," I replied.

Apparently Melville could fly the airplane as long as that was all he had to do, but when he was loaded up, he didn't react. I could not see an easy way around the problem. I should have told Melville that he was not suited to become a pilot but I remembered that he had said he would be happy to just go on his first solo flight.

Back on the ground, I asked Melville if he could come for his lesson the next day at 15:00 instead of 15:30.

15

"Sure. Why?"

"Don't ask. Just be here."

"Okay."

On Wednesday, I sent Melville solo. He came early, I hustled him out to the airplane. We took off and he showed me three good circuits. There were three other training aircraft in the pattern with us and Melville had no trouble following the radio work. On the fourth round I called for a full stop landing and had Melville pull off the runway. I picked up the microphone and announced on the tower frequency that this student was going on his first solo and the instructor would be walking in from the side of the runway. As soon as I replaced the microphone, the radio jammed with activity.

"Delta India Uniform is leaving the circuit for a local flight, tower."

"X-ray Tango Gulf is doing a full stop on this one."

"November India Quebec is departing the circuit southwest."

All three airplanes bailed out of the circuit.

"Well, Melville, you're on your own," I said. "I want you to fly one circuit with a full stop landing. The airplane will fly lighter without me in it, so don't be surprised when it pops off the runway during the takeoff. Keep up the good work and I'll see you back at the office."

"Okay, boss." Melville's tongue was at maximum hang, but he was smiling.

I watched him do a good takeoff and then I walked to the flying school to listen to his radio work on the office monitor.

The tower controller was the first one to speak. "Tango Victor Hotel, where are you going?"

No reply.

"TANGO VICTOR HOTEL, WHERE ARE YOU GOING?"

No reply.

"MELVILLE, WHERE ARE YOU GOING?"

This time he got a response, but it wasn't the one I wanted to hear.

"I'm goin' to fly over the farm."

"Oh no he's not," I said to myself. I picked up the direct line to the control tower. While it was ringing, I heard the tower suggest that Melville come back to the circuit.

"I'm just goin' to fly over the farm."

It was several rings before anyone answered. "Hi, this is Melville's instructor. Tell him that I order him to return at once."

"Okay, but he sounds determined."

They told him what I said and got no reply.

"Tango Victor Hotel, Derry Tower, do you read?"

No reply.

"MELVILLE, DO YOU HEAR US?"

No reply.

The controller came back on the phone. "What's your next idea?"

"Tell Melville that if he doesn't turn back immediately, I will be waiting for him with his father's pig castrators."

"I don't think we can say that on the air."

"Well, that's my best idea, what's yours?"

"We'll try it."

"Tango Victor, I mean Melville, your instructor said that if you don't turn around right now, he will be waiting for you with certain pig appliances belonging to your father."

No reply.

"Melville, what I mean is, when you do come back, your instructor will make sure you spend the rest of your life talking in a high voice. Do you understand?"

"Yes, I think so," Melville replied.

"Are you turning around, now?"

"Yes."

"Good. Call me when you're on the downwind leg."

A round of cheers went up in the flying school from the small group of staff that had gathered around the monitor, but they were cut short by three successive calls from the afternoon's inbound regional airliners. I thought it was over for Melville and my instructing career. The controller saved the day.

"I need the three of you to widen out your approaches. Melville is joining the downwind on his first solo." It worked. The airline pilots were regulars at the Derry Airport.

"No problem, tower."

"Same for us, tower. Way to go Melville."

"Congratulations Melville."

He made it down okay. I decided to hold the tough talk and let him enjoy the rituals of the first solo. After all, now I wouldn't have to fly with him again.

He grinned while I hit him with a bucket of water and cut his shirt to hang on the wall.

When the excitement was over, he pumped my hand and said. "When do we go again? I wanna get my licence and I don't wanna fly with anyone else but you."

Chapter Three

Country squire

"I found it," Susan exclaimed in a gush of little girl excitement.

I was immediately worried. Susan was not a little girl. In two years of marriage she had acted like this only twice before. The first time was when she quit her fashion buyer's job to clean stalls for $5 a day and the other time was when she bought a horse.

Susan was picking me up at the end of a day at Derry Air. She had been looking for a place for us to live. We had decided to buy a small starter home rather than paying rent. We didn't have any money but the government was running a "stimulate the economy" scheme where it loaned the down payment to first time home buyers who qualified for a regular mortgage except for the fact they didn't have any money.

This had been Susan's third day looking. I was not surprised that she had found something already. Susan was someone who made decisions easily and quickly.

"Great?" I said. The tone of my voice carried the question mark. I climbed into the right seat of our old Volkswagen Beetle. Lady, our German Shepherd, leaned forward from the back seat and washed the left side of my head. "Hello, Lady. Hello Susan. Tell me about the house."

"I think you're going to like it, but it's not what we first discussed," she said quickly.

"When did we second discuss?" I asked. I had learned that my only hope of keeping up to Susan at a time like this was to stay on the offensive.

"Do you want to see it?" she asked, ignoring my question. Her look told me to say "yes".

"It's getting dark," I said.

"I bought a flashlight," she replied pulling a 69-cent disposable plastic light from her purse. She pointed it in my face and turned it on.

"Okay, Sherlock, anything you say."

"Good. Lady and I both think this place is perfect."

I realized if majority ruled in this family, a decision had been made already.

Up to that point I had failed to notice two significant things. We were stopped for no reason at the exit of the Derry Air parking lot and Susan was wearing a new suit. When she had dropped me off that morning, she didn't own a new suit.

She turned left. The city of Derry was to the right.

"Where are we going?" I asked.

"Well, I know we talked about buying a little starter house in town so we could still afford for you to take multi-engine flying, but that would mean boarding Cricket in the country and travelling back and forth to ride."

Cricket was her horse.

"So it occurred to me that we could save money by buying a little place outside of the city where we could keep Cricket with us."

"And I could drive back and forth to work?"

"We can both drive back and forth to work."

"You don't have a job."

"I start Monday at the Fashion and Designer Emporium in the East End Mall."

"You got a job today? I thought you were looking for a house?"

"I found the house this morning," she said, sounding very business-like. "This afternoon I got a job selling ladies wear. I phoned my old boss, Hymie Waumbaum and he put me on to Norbert Bronze. He owns a chain of these ladies wear stores. I was interviewed by the East End store manager an hour ago and I start as a sales clerk Monday morning."

Life with Susan was never dull.

"Do we move into our new house tonight using that flashlight?" I asked.

"We could. It's empty."

"So we bought it already?"

"No, you're being silly. I wouldn't do that before you had a chance to see it. We can look tonight. If you like it, I'll buy it tomorrow."

"So we're going to look at a little place in the country. How long has it been abandoned?"

"It's not abandoned, just empty and it's not little. I discovered that there are no little places in the country."

"How unlittle is it?"

"It's an older farm house with some outbuildings on a few acres of pasture. There is a beautiful stream running beside it. Cricket can have a place in one of the barns and can roam a section of pasture. The rest of the land will provide hay for the winter. The real estate agent said local farmers would rent some of the land and buildings."

"And this place is in our budget?"

"My salary will cover the extra cost. That's why I got a job."

"How much extra are we talking about?"

"Thirty-five acres."

"The house?"

"Five bedrooms, 3,000 square feet."

"The outbuildings?"

"It was a working dairy farm up to six months ago with 50 head of cattle."

"And we're going to pay for this with the addition of your salary?"

"It will be tight at first. I'll need my own car because our work hours don't match and the new place will need a few things such as decorating, furniture, insurance, windows and fence but we'll manage. We always have."

At this point, I knew that I was being driven by a force more powerful than me: my wife. We had been married long enough that I knew it was best to go along for the ride.

We had been driving for a long time. It was dark and I didn't have a clue where we were.

"How far away is this place?"

"We're about halfway. There was nothing close to town near our price range." Susan shifted into her sales mode. "I know you haven't had time to think about living in the country but I'd like you to look at this place and then we can talk. The more I think about it, the more I like the idea of being away from the city, living in the fresh air, friendly neighbours, open fields and a place for horses."

I was tired, but I didn't miss the "s" on horses.

"It will be a healthier place for us," she continued, "and it will be a good investment. You'll make a fine country squire."

I wasn't sure what a country squire was but I knew there were other things I wanted to be.

20

"Does the 35 acres happen to be long and flat, have a windsock in the middle and a hangar next to the house?"

"No. You never mentioned wanting a landing strip in the country, so I didn't look for one."

Susan stopped at an intersection in a little village named Cranberry. I counted ten houses and three churches. There were no stores.

"The place we're looking at is on this next road about four kilometres away."

As we left Cranberry, the farm houses were spaced about half a kilometre apart. Except for yard lights, they were dark.

"These places are all abandoned," I said.

"No, they're dairy farms. It's nine o'clock and everyone has gone to bed."

It was hard to tell in the dark, but the terrain looked flat. A landing strip might work.

"This is it coming up on the right."

The buildings were close to the road. As Susan pulled into the driveway, I could make out the silhouette of at least two barns on the right and a large house on the left. She parked in between with the VW headlights on the largest barn.

"What do you think?" she asked.

"Bring that search light and let's have a look."

The three of us climbed out of the car. Susan pointed her flashlight at a small block building beside the barn.

"Milkhouse?" I said.

"It was," she replied. "It'll be the tack room."

She opened the side door to the large barn. Her little light was unable to penetrate very far through the maze of cobwebs that hung in sheets from the low ceiling but I could see a row of cow stanchions, watering bowls and a ditch. Under the cob webs, layers of whitewash were caked on and flaking off. Chunks of it crunched under our feet.

"Spider farm," I said.

She didn't answer. I followed Susan to an opening for another barn that was attached on the other side. I could feel Lady pressing against my leg.

"The ceiling in this part is too low for horses," Susan said, "but over here it's okay. This is where the cows must have been kept for breeding."

She shone her light through the door into a more open area containing large holding pens.

21

"Upstairs," she said pointing her light at the ceiling, "is the hay loft."

"Is that where Lady and I sleep?"

"No. Lady sleeps with me. Come on, I'll show you the house."

We walked across the yard to a two-storey, clapboard house. Susan climbed the three steps to a wooden porch.

"Do you have a key?"

She turned the knob and opened the door. "This is the country. There are no locks."

Inside was an empty, reasonably clean but well-worn monument to the 1950s. Susan shone her light around acres of blond-colored imitation wood paneling, warped acoustic ceiling tiles and sloping hardwood floors. A huge eat-in kitchen was decorated with pink and black plastic tiles, blue and green painted plywood cupboards and broken turquoise and white asphalt squares on the floor. There was an equally huge cement-floored summer kitchen out back. The dining room was covered with red brocade wallpaper. Upstairs, there were five bedrooms with curling wallpaper unsuccessfully holding plaster and lath onto the walls. The bathroom was actually a small converted sixth bedroom with bright turquoise fixtures.

"I know we can't afford to redecorate and furnish all of this but we don't have to." Her voice echoed off the bare walls. "We'll just do the few rooms we need for the three of us."

It was obvious that Susan had made up her mind about buying this place. From experience I knew that it was my job to either find a really good reason not to or get excited and say yes.

"Is there a basement?"

"No. The real estate agent said that the house sits on logs on the ground."

"Water?"

"Pumped from a cistern connected to the eaves troughs."

"Sewer?"

"Septic bed out the side."

"Heat?"

"That's the best part. Space heaters are fed by a natural gas well across the road on property that was part of this farm." She pointed her light at an old cast iron contraption on the floor about the size of a bread box. I had never seen one before. "The real estate agent said we have free use of the gas well."

"Roof?"

"Steel. I can't wait to hear the patter of rain drops on it."

"How do we know that this place isn't about to fall down?"

"Good question. The real estate agent said that it's been here for over 100 years and probably would be for another 100."

"Well, why don't we think about it and come back when I have time off next week and we can see it during daylight?"

"Two reasons: I'll be working and it may be sold. This place is part of an estate sale. It has been empty for six months but it only came on the market yesterday. The real estate agent said that the local farmers have their eyes on it for the land. They will jump as soon as he puts his "For Sale" sign up tomorrow."

"Well, I'm sure what he said is mostly salesmanship. Are we not being rushed into this? It can't be the only farm for sale in the area."

"You're being rushed into this. I'm quite happy. This place is available now for the price of the land and I like it. I could keep looking around or we could stop operating out of a suitcase and get on with living. It's Thursday. That gives me Friday to arrange the mortgage and the down payment. I start work on Monday. You can move us in on your first day off next week."

I couldn't see her face in the dark, but I didn't have to. Her voice had "say yes" written all over it.

"What's this place called?"

"YAHOOOOO!" she yelled and grabbed me in a bear hug. Her exclamation echoed around the whole house. "I knew you'd like it. You won't regret this. Come on. Let's go find some supper and celebrate."

She and Lady disappeared out the front door.

I stood in the dark feeling mostly numb. I wondered what it would be like to go from being broke and living out of a suitcase to being a debt-ridden land baron.

"What the hell," I said to the empty house.

Susan thundered back up the porch steps and stuck her head in the door.

"It's called Windy Acres." she said.

Chapter Four

Fritz

The maintenance shop at Derry Air was on the opposite side of the hangar from the flight department. Sending Melville on his first solo had made me instantly famous with the other instructing staff, but after a week on the job, I had not been on the other side of the hangar to meet Derry Air's mechanics.

Nobody had warned me about Fritz. Fritz was the avionics technician. The first time I saw him, he burst into the flight lounge looking for a pilot. It was lunch hour and I was the only instructor around. This wild looking mechanic charged in my direction, his open white lab coat flowing behind him, acid holes, solder globs, pen streaks and all. He was the perfect picture of the mad scientist. His bushy brows topped a pair of wide eyes. His salt and pepper hair defied gravity in all directions.

I found out later that Fritz was a European immigrant who had been in the country 14 years. He was fluent in four languages, none of them English.

He stuck his face in mine and said, "Cum, you fly wit me."

He turned and started away, motioning impatiently for me to follow.

"I have a student in 40 minutes," I said.

"No questions!" he replied excitedly. "We test Navidjoe."

Until then I had not moved, but now I was interested. I thought I recognized the word 'Navajo', as in Piper Navajo, the high performance twin-engined aircraft in Derry Air's charter department. It was the main reason I had joined the company.

"Do you want me to fly with you in the Navajo?" I asked.

"No questions!" he yelled back and disappeared out the door.

If this mechanic was inviting me on a Navajo test flight, then I was game. I chased after him and gained the airside apron in time to see him climb into the company Navajo. I trotted up to the rear airstair door and stuck my head inside. There was a flurry of elbows coming from the left cockpit seat. The right engine started.

I climbed in.

The left engine started.

I closed the door.

The wild man released the brakes and applied power.

I struggled up the narrow aisle against the rapid acceleration and hauled myself into the right seat. We were charging off toward the runways at a hasty clip. I donned the copilot's headset in time to hear this mad pilot call the control tower.

"Derry One, ready de takeoft."

He didn't use the aircraft registration letters, just "Derry One." We hadn't done a run-up or any pre-takeoff checks. The runway was still some distance away, but the guy was adding more power.

"Derry One is cleared for takeoff Runway 06, wind 300 at 10," the controller replied.

The only response was the application of full power. The tires screeched as we roared around the corner onto the runway. After an impossibly short run, the pilot yanked the control wheel back. The Navajo staggered into the air.

My breathing stopped. I didn't think the airplane would stay up at such an impossibly slow speed.

The pilot snapped the landing gear lever up. My heart stopped. Now if the Navajo sank, we were going to flop down on the propellers.

For a long time the airplane hung over the runway locked in an aerodynamic stalemate with gravity. The two engines were howling at full power. Finally the airspeed began to increase, one knot at a time. When we passed the end of the runway, the airplane started to gain altitude. I didn't know who this man was, but he flew worse than my worst student.

I started breathing again and looked around the cockpit. The pilot motioned for me to take over control. Without waiting to see if I had, he rolled his seat back, turned completely around, stuck his feet in the air and worked his torso under the instrument panel.

"Turn on zee hautopilot," he yelled.

It took me a minute to find the autopilot while teaching myself to fly the airplane. We were still climbing with the engines at full power. I turned the autopilot on. The control wheel immediately slammed to full left aileron, taking my arm with it. The Navajo obediently launched into a roll to the left. Approaching a 60 degree bank, I forced the control wheel toward neutral. I didn't know if I should be forcing anything, but it seemed like a better idea than going inverted. I pulled back on the control wheel to prevent the airplane from going into a spiral. The engines were still set at full power, 300 horsepower per side. The Navajo obediently circled in a tight steep turn.

I could hear muttering in some other language coming from under the panel. There were sounds of electrical arcing. A few sparks bounced off the guy's chest and then suddenly the autopilot's roll command stopped. The control wheel slammed to full right aileron from the force I was applying to it. The aircraft began righting itself.

The pilot crawled out with a satisfied look on his face. He turned in his seat and took over control.

"All fixed," he said with a grin. He turned the Navajo back toward the airport, pointed the nose down and called the tower. The engines were still at full power.

"Derry One is ready zee landing," he said into the microphone.

The controller seemed unconcerned about the man's lack of proper radio procedure. "Derry One, roger, you're cleared to land Runway 24, wind 300 at 10, check gear down."

There was no reply. The Navajo was aimed for the beginning of the runway. We were doing over 200 knots and the speed was increasing. When we were a mile from touchdown, I suspected the pilot might drive this beautiful airplane onto the runway at high speed with the wheels up and me in it. His hand wasn't on the throttles, so I reached over and pulled them back to idle. The "low power/wheels up" warning horn immediately sounded.

"Vas is dis?" he shouted.

Before I answered, I put my hand over the landing gear lever. I thought if the wheels were extended at high speed, they might rip off. "It's the wheels up horn," I yelled back. "Raise the nose and slow down."

He reached for the gear lever, but got my hand instead. The Navajo continued pointed at the runway. With my other hand I could feel he had an iron grip on the control wheel. I used the electric pitch trim to raise our nose. We went sailing over the end of the runway. It was a mile long, so we had plenty of room.

When I thought we had slowed down enough, I lowered the gear. The pilot continued to push the control wheel forward, trying to force the airplane onto the runway. I continued to counteract with up trim. The resulting porpoise must have looked interesting from outside. His control forces must have been enormous.

"Vas is dis?" he said, looking at the controls. He began stabbing at the autopilot buttons. The distraction allowed the airplane time to slow down. With a few skips and jumps, the Navajo eventually settled onto the runway. The pilot steered us onto the taxiway at speed and headed for the ramp without calling ground control.

I was mad. I didn't appreciate being terrorized by a crazed mechanic who for some reason decided to turn an autopilot test flight into a death wish. I didn't even know the man's name.

"Whoever you are, you have a real problem," I said after we had stopped. "I don't know where you learned to fly, but I think you were trying to kill us!"

The guy stopped midway out of his seat and looked at me with wide eyes.

"I don't know you edder," he said, "but I never learnt to fly. You're da pilote. I tought you try to kill me!"

With that he disappeared down the aisle and out the door.

Chapter Five

HALO

Derry Air's chief flying instructor, Eric Daedalus, had a laugh-a-minute personality and a roly-poly body to match. He ran the flying school with a grin. He believed that it was unnecessary to elaborate on the learn-to-fly standards established by the government. He made sure each instructor followed the government curriculum and that they were happy. His lighthearted attitude was a welcome buffer between the instructors and the flying school's scar-faced owner, Irving Mingy.

When I started at Derry Air, Eric met with me regularly but informally. He laughed at everything, including Mingy's sinister nature. "He's not really that bad, when you get to know him," Eric said to me one day over coffee. "He's worse," he added and then roared at his own joke.

Eric had one of those laughs that started as an infectious belly chuckle that grew into an outright roar when it reached the top. Whenever you saw him, you couldn't help smiling. You knew a laugh was coming soon.

Another time when Eric and I were waiting for the weather to improve, I asked him how Derry Air began and how he came to work for Mingy.

"Irv and I met in the army," he said and then chuckled. "When you've been in the military for a while, you can make friends with anyone."

He smiled and said that Mingy mustered out of the army first and started Derry Air.

"When I was discharged, I didn't know what I wanted to do so Irv asked me to come here and teach flying. He paid for my training and here I am. I still don't know what I'm doing," he added and then laughed some more.

"What happened to Mingy's face?" I asked.

"Skydiving for beers," Eric answered. "He was an army paratrooper." Eric chuckled to himself. The question had obviously revived an old memory.

"He was practicing a HALO drop, a high-altitude free fall with a low opening parachute. The technique was designed for jumps behind enemy lines. Mingy bet a buddy a beer that he would open last.

"Down they went, each one holding the override on the automatic opener, waiting for the other guy to chicken out. The crazy buggers waited too long. Irv's chute was just starting to pop when he hit. Fortunately he landed in a small lake, but the water rammed into his helmet and ripped it off. The chin strap shattered his jaw."

Eric laughed between each sentence as he told the story. I sat there with my mouth open. Knowing Mingy a little made the story believable.

"Did he win?" I asked.

"Ya, he won big — the beer and a medical discharge. He started Derry Air after the military rebuilt his face and let him out with a bag of money. That's why you and I are flying with these students and he's the owner.

"It's a good story," I said. "It makes him seem a little more human. How long did you know Mingy before he told you that one?"

"He never told me," Eric laughed and started to get up from the table. "He didn't have to; I was the buddy. I opened first and wasn't hurt. I had to buy the beer and stay in the army for four more years."

Still smiling, Eric said, "Come on, it's clearing up, let's go flying."

Chapter Six

Dutch

"Remember, da ADF reading plus da heading equals your position 'TO' da station, except ven da number is over 360, den subtract 360, ya?"

Dutch VanDerHoven was briefing on aviation's worst invention, the fixed-card Automatic Direction Finder. He was using an oversized replica of the face of an ADF indicator complete with pointer. The student's eyes were well glazed indicating that he was not working on all cylinders.

Dutch continued. He was showing a patience that can only come from years of teaching. "Vell, get in da box and ve try it," he said, motioning to the simulator at the back of the classroom.

Dutch was Derry Air's ground instructor. He was a short, stocky fireplug of a man in his mid-fifties. The brush cut, crisp clothes and erect stance were a product of many proud years in the air force. Dutch had flown F-86 Sabre jet fighters until one that he was in caught fire.

"I tried diving to put out da flames. It didn't vork. Den I was going too fast to punch out."

Dutch ejected anyway. His compact body survived the near supersonic wind blast, but the sudden pressure ruptured an eardrum. "I shouldn't 'ave turned to vatch me go."

Dutch stayed in the air force as a ground instructor until retiring at age 45. Then Derry Air owner Irving Mingy hired him to run the classroom. Everybody liked Dutch. He possessed an infectious enthusiasm for aviation and a marvelously indiscreet way of teaching it, but he was having trouble with this student.

I was the student. Dutch was giving me ground instruction in instrument flying. The training was my first step toward an Instrument Rating on multi-engine aircraft. I had made a deal with Dutch to give me these after-hour simulator lessons in exchange for a flying refresher course. Dutch had decided to get a civilian Commercial Pilot Licence. The government had changed the medical requirements recently to allow pilots deaf in one ear to fly commercially.

This lesson was being given at the end of a long day for both of us. I had been instructing a succession of Derry Air student pilots and now I was having trouble concentrating.

Dutch rapped my head with his knuckles as I settled into the simulator. "Yust remember, da angle of da dangle equals da heat of da meat, ya?" he said with a chuckle.

Dutch had built the Derry Air simulator himself. It was made from the wreck of an eight-passenger Aero Commander 500. Dutch had cut the cockpit off the fuselage behind the bulkhead separating it from the passenger compartment. There was a pilot door on the left, but the windows were covered over with aluminum. The controls activated the instruments through a computer. The Derry Air mechanics had stenciled "Dutch Air Force" above a rough drawing of a little boy with something other than his finger in a dike. The whole cockpit was bolted to the floor which made me skeptical about the contraption's ability to simulate anything other than claustrophobia. On Dutch's desk there was a repeater instrument panel and a crab-like contraption that traced an outline of the theoretical flight on a sheet of Plexiglas laid on top of an aeronautical chart of the area.

"I'll leave da door open and valk you t'ru da first lesson," Dutch said.

He stood beside the simulator and showed me how it worked. We did some Automatic Direction Finding position fixes with the pitch and roll functions locked out. I tuned different Non-Directional Beacon stations and electronically turned the airplane using the rudder pedals. I had taught these maneuvers to students on the Commercial Pilot course. I couldn't help thinking the "box" wasn't contributing much to my IFR education. I made the mistake of voicing that opinion.

"This doesn't feel like instrument flying, Dutch." It was a mental lapse on my part.

Dutch turned red. "Put your headset on," he said. Then he closed the simulator door.

As my eyes adjusted to the dim glow of the instrument lighting, I found the headset.

Dutch's voice crackled over the intercom. "Climb to 4,000 feet, turn to 210 degrees and tune da Derry NDB." He didn't speak again for ten minutes.

For a few seconds I was okay, like when you first stand on a beach ball. Then the simulator's equilibrium slipped away from me. Dutch had rigged the instruments and controls to be overly sensitive. Since I was sitting in the dark in a cockpit bolted to the floor, I was robbed of any sense of motion. Visually, I had to rely on the instruments. Right now they were telling me bad things. I was losing control of this "airplane". I took stabs at correcting, but every action produced a reaction of several magnitudes. I would concentrate on getting the wings level and discover I was in a dive. I would pull up and the airplane would roll. I would counteract and find the airplane climbing madly. I was thrashing around the cockpit like an octopus directing traffic. I hadn't even looked at the ADF, as ordered.

"Vat is da ADF reading?" Dutch asked.

It was still spinning.

"Which time?" I replied.

He let me fight with the simulator for another five minutes. My perspiration made the control wheel slippery. Every time I gained on one thing, I'd lose the others, but the gyrations were coming in diminishing proportions as I slowly adjusted to the simulator's sensitivity.

He finally opened the simulator door and said. "Velcome to instrument flying, Hotshot. T'ink you can learn anyt'ing in dere?"

"Yes sir," I said with a sigh.

"Good. Next time ve go a little slower, ya?"

"You're the boss."

Chapter Seven

Double jeopardy

The next morning Susan dropped me off at work at 6:30 a.m. I had arranged to fly with Dutch on his first refresher lesson in the air. Walking from the parking lot, I felt cold and sleepy. It was too soon to be back on the job after the previous night but I didn't have any choice. Dutch had worked a special deal with stingy Mingy to rent the aircraft for a discount before eight a.m.

I arrived in time to witness Derry Air's line crew, Huey, Duey and Louey, using the company's new avgas refueling tanker to push start the older jet fuel truck. The three linemen were part of two shifts at Derry Air that serviced the ten flying school airplanes as well as the Navajo and Aztec in the charter fleet, the customer aircraft and the visiting airline flights. Huey, Duey and Louey were not their real names but the three gangly teenagers always followed each other around in single file. I don't know who nick-named them but it was obvious why it stuck.

As I walked toward the office, I watched as Huey eased the shiny new truck against the back of the old tanker being driven by Duey. Huey revved the engine and popped the clutch. Nothing moved. The drive wheels just spun on the frosty ramp. Louey fixed this problem with the linecrew trick of melting ice with fuel. He pumped a few dozen litres of avgas onto the ramp in front of the tires.

Huey backed the truck up a few feet and took a short running bump into the dead truck. This got both vehicles moving between the rows of parked airplanes. When they reached a good speed, Duey popped the clutch on the jet truck. He was rewarded with a momentary burst of life from the engine. This opened a gap between the two tankers, but then the engine on the jet truck died. The rear wheels locked.

At first the surge of fuel in the tank carried the jet truck further forward, but then the mass rolled back, stopping the tanker in its tracks. Huey, in the avgas bowser, reacted as quickly as any teenager could at six-thirty in the morning. He drove straight into the back of the other truck. The impact left the outline of the new truck in the tank of the old and started both loads of fuel surging in different directions. The two vehicles hopped and banged themselves together down the ramp in a series of decreasing collisions. They looked like a drunken mechanical inchworm.

The new truck was badly damaged. Smoke rose from the engine and fluid was leaking from underneath. Huey, Duey and Louey ran from the wrecks. I wondered if the two trucks would blow up or just start a monster fire. The air traffic controller in the tower had been watching and called out the airport crash truck. The rescue crew foamed both tankers, adding a surreal frosting to the whole mess.

Dutch VanDerHoven arrived with Darcy Philips, Derry Air's chief mechanic. Dutch took command right away. He collared a wide-eyed Huey and asked him what had happened. It took a few minutes for the excited teenager to relate the story. I was standing nearby and could hear that he was giving it to him straight. In the meantime, Darcy checked out the trucks and reported back to Dutch.

"The jet truck is okay except for the mother dent in the back. It won't run because it's out of gas. The new one is toast until we get another rad and front end parts."

"Okay, here is vat ve gonna do," Dutch said. There were seven of us standing in a loose circle listening to him: the three linecrew, myself, Darcy, and the two firefighters. "I need you two boys," he said to the firefighters, "to hose all dat foam off da trucks. Huey, you go to da fuel farm and get some auto gas for da jet truck. Back it into da parking spot so ve can't see da rear. Duey and Louey, I vant all da front end parts off dat odder truck before Mingy gets here in vun hour. Darcy vill show you how. Da story stays da same but if ve clean up dis mess, it don't look so bad. Ve change vun t'ing. Da truck is out of gas because somevun syphoned it last night. I speak to Angel to fix da fuel sheets."

"You," he said pointing to me, "you and I go flying."

Dutch's handling of the situation was opposite to what I had expected. I thought he would have chewed out the three line boys thoroughly and left them in Mingy's office for him to do worse.

I followed Dutch into the office. He spoke quietly to Angel and came away with the log book and keys for the aircraft we were going to use for our flying lesson.

"Okay, Hotshot," he said to me, "ve are signed out, let's go."

When we had cleared the door, I said, "Dutch, tell me what you were doing for the linecrew."

"Sure," he said, marching toward our airplane. "I tell you vile I doing da valkaround."

He opened the door to the Cherokee, extended its flaps and climbed back out with the fuel sample jar in his hand.

"You see," he said while checking the condition of the right wing, "Irv gets upset ven somet'ing like dis happens, especially ven it cost him money. But dose boys are not to blame, Irv is. Everybody needs teaching to do da job. Irv is too cheap to train da boys so dey screw up. It's not der fault. So I help dem smood t'ings out. Ve do da same in da air force."

Dutch's comments were a further insight into the man's complex and kindly character. I was feeling badly for what I had planned to do to him to get even for his making my life miserable in the simulator. I had booked the school's oldest Cherokee 140; the one that had seen too many spiral recoveries and hard landings; the one that entered a wicked spin every time it was stalled no matter what the pilot did. I was going to have Dutch practise wing stalls knowing that the inevitable spin would scare the life out of him.

It was too late to change airplanes so I decided we would avoid stalls for this first lesson. We took off and headed toward Derry harbor along the lakeshore, just outside the Derry control zone. I started Dutch with basic climbs, descents and turns. He was good. Most students flying after a long layoff are ham-handed at first, but Dutch didn't show any of that. He completed each of the simple maneuvers easily and expertly. I had him try some steep turns and slow flight maneuvers. Cherokees wallow easily at low speed but Dutch controlled that well. It was obvious that I was wasting his time.

"You're doing fine, Dutch, let's head back to the airport and practise some takeoffs and landings."

"See dat ship?" he said, nodding his head toward the harbor below.

I looked down in that direction. A large, black-hulled lake freighter was steaming toward the docks.

"Yes," I answered. I didn't have a clue what was going to

35

happen next.

We were flying at low speed with engine power on. Dutch snapped the Cherokee's nose up and booted full left rudder. The airplane rolled over onto its back and continued into the almightiest spin I had ever seen.

"I've got it," I yelled as accumulated dirt and lost pencils floated past our faces. I looked at Dutch. He was grinning. I tried my controls. They wouldn't budge. Dutch was holding the airplane in the spin.

"I've got control," I yelled again.

There was no response. I tried to push the control wheel, but was no match for Dutch's iron grip. We were starting our third revolution and passing through 3,000 feet when Dutch finally spoke again.

"Ven I started in da Air Force," he said calmly, still holding the spin, "I flew Avenger torpedo bombers."

I was afraid he had lost his mind. We passed 2,000 feet. "Let go, Dutch," I yelled in his ear.

"Ven ve attack a ship, ve fool da gunners," he continued. "Ve make dem t'ink ve are spinning out of control like now."

At that moment he stuffed the wheel forward and punched opposite rudder. The spin stopped. We were pointed straight at the harbor in a vertical dive.

"Den ve recover at da last second," he said, still grinning.

He hauled back on the controls and leveled off inches above the water. The words, "Canada Steamship Lines", crossed our windshield dead ahead.

"Right about HERE," he said, stabbing at an imaginary button on his control wheel, "ve drop da fish."

He pulled up in time to clear the deck in front of the bridge. Then he dove for the surface again, executing irregular S-turns to evade imaginary enemy fire.

My heart was beating in my throat and the fingers on both my hands hurt. My right hand was gripping the control wheel and my left hand was imprinting the plastic of the glare shield on top of the instrument panel.

I wanted to get mad but I was having trouble. Dutch had scared the hell out of me but I was the one who had given him the opportunity. He had broken several air regulations but had performed the maneuver without overstressing the airplane. It was unlikely anyone on the ship caught our registration as we flashed by at eye level.

I relaxed my grip as Dutch climbed away from the harbor. "Dat vas fun," he said calmly. He eyed the shoreline and pushed forward on the controls. "Do you vant to see how ve strafe da beach?"

"No!" I screamed and grabbed for the controls.

"Okay," he said, pulling up once more. "Vat do you vant to do now?"

"Let's go back to the airport and you can show me a landing," I said.

His face lit up. "Like on the aircraft carrier?"

"No!" I screamed again. "Like a normal full stop landing on the runway. I've had too much excitement already today."

"Okay." He looked disappointed.

"Dutch, as long as we're flying together," I said, "will you ever do anything like that again?"

"Not if you don't vant," he said.

"I don't vant," I replied.

"You're da boss."

Chapter Eight

Windy Acres

Susan and I bought the place near Cranberry. A lawyer closed the deal at the end of the month and we became the proud owners of a 35 acre farm with seven buildings and two mortgages.

My second look at "Windy Acres" was my first in daylight. It will be the last farm I purchase at night.

The land in that area was flat except for ours. The neighbouring farms were perfect potential airports but a stream ran through Windy Acres. It cut the land into picturesque rolling ridges. There wasn't a 500-foot flat piece anywhere. Susan and I didn't have an airplane but it didn't seem right for a pilot to own 35 acres on which it would have been difficult to land a helicopter.

The buildings included a large L-shaped barn, a smaller barn, a pig shed, a chicken coop, a smokehouse, a milkhouse and a farmhouse. They were all clustered on a high spot of land in one corner of the acreage. Each building was in a different stage of disrepair.

In many ways, the house was the worst. There was evidence that it had been white, but the paint had long since peeled or faded leaving greying clapboard. The arrangement of the rolling land funneled the prevailing wind toward the house where a venturi effect provided a constant breeze. This caused the loose clapboard to clap, continuously. It also rattled the old windows in their rotting frames and made the rusted metal roof heave up and down in great creaking sighs.

It didn't take us too long to discover a few other reasons why the real estate agent must have been happy to meet a couple of city folk.

The prevailing wind blew from the manure pile at the end of the large barn. This put a new meaning into the expression "fresh air". To a farmer it might have been perfume but Susan and I prayed for east winds until we found someone to haul the pile away.

The house sat on logs instead of a basement. The structure rose and fell regularly and unevenly with the change in seasons.

This popped windows and skewed door frames. I learned the hard way why there were no locks on the doors. I installed one but after a couple of months the bolt didn't line up with the receiver.

During our first rainfall, the steel roof provided Susan with enough pitter-patter to last a lifetime. There was no insulation in the house, so the raindrops sounded like a thousand sticks beating on a steel drum in which we were occupants. The rain also awakened us to the fact that a heaving roof leaks. Every time the wind blew, which was always, it lifted the steel sheets and pulled the nails holding them down. It was a regular sight to see me crawling across the roof with a mouthful of nails, a hammer, a brush and a bucket of pitch.

We initially loved having the soft rain water from the cistern until we discovered what comes with it. It didn't take a magnifying glass to see the assorted bugs, leaves, rust and bird bombings in a glass of our water. I tried keeping the eaves troughs clean but eventually gave up and paid a local trucker to dump city water into our cistern.

The free heat from the natural gas well across the road was my most educational country experience. The well was there and many of our neighbours had one like it. From them we learned that the condensation must be pumped from the well regularly or it caused the sides to collapse. Properly maintained, the well would provide us with low pressure gas via a two kilometre-long antique iron pipe that ran under the road through the culvert carrying the stream. Occasionally the gas would blow holes through the side of the rusty pipe where it lay in the stream. This would be announced by a geyser of gas-propelled water erupting from the surface.

What gas did reach the house was fed into three cast iron antique space heaters, two downstairs and one upstairs. When lit, they produced a tiny row of flames along the bottom of the fixture. Susan and I tried them our first night on the farm. The heat given off was modest. When the weather turned colder, the pressure in the well dropped and the heat could no longer keep up with the breezes blowing though the house. On the really frigid days, there wasn't enough pressure to keep the gas lit. There was nothing we could do except shut them off and move to a hotel in Derry. Every time we did this the plumbing froze. The neighbours told us that the previous owners kept warm by having kids, thirteen of them. Susan and I bought an oil furnace.

All those problems were still ahead of us the day we moved into the house. Susan had bought candles, wine and sandwiches for a romantic dinner that night. We carried the kitchen table into the livingroom to be in front of the space heater. We sat in the midst of

DERRY AIR

a pile of our possessions and naively toasted our good fortune.

Chapter Nine

Angel

The best thing that ever happened to Derry Air was Angel. Her job title was receptionist but in reality she ran the air service. Angel roosted on her stool behind the flight desk and controlled everything. She greeted each customer, answered the phone, signed out all flights, arranged the aircraft maintenance and made sure everyone paid.

Angel possessed a steel trap mind. She never used a cash register or calculator. She entered the flight times in the Aircraft Journey and Maintenance log books and remembered the times to inspection and overhaul for each one. She knew the distance from Derry to Peoria, Illinois, and most other towns in a 500 nautical mile radius from preparing charter quotes. Angel remembered the last time each rental customer had flown. She was never wrong.

Angel's disposition was mostly neutral. She was friendly enough but was not interested in idle conversation. She was well liked for her efficiency. In appearance, nature had dealt her a cruel hand. Angel resembled the offspring of a witch and a wrestler. She was shaped like a large mound of melting ice cream topped with short straight hair. She dressed in cheap moo moos and red running shoes. The haphazard arrangement of her remaining teeth played havoc with a smile that she rarely used.

Angel was devoted to her job. She was a wallflower who had discovered something satisfying she could do well in the real world. Derry Air saved her from staying home with her parents, putting up preserves, knitting for the homeless and terrifying single men at socials.

When I started instructing at Derry Air, Angel assigned me students right from the first day; I just had to be there waiting. That's what I was doing when Robert Redford walked into the office.

It was the real Robert Redford, the movie star. To be in Derry, he must have taken a wrong turn off Hollywood Boulevard and slipped through the Twilight Zone. I found out later that he flew his own airplane and was on his way to the Toronto Film Festival.

He had stopped at Derry Airport to clear customs and refuel.

I recognized him right away. Susan had dragged me to every movie the blond grin specialist had made. From the other side of the lounge I could see that Redford carried his good looks and easy manner off the screen. I stayed in my seat to watch the iron maiden of Derry Air dissolve into a puddle when she realized who was approaching her counter. It didn't occur to me that church-going wallflower daughters of Ukrainian immigrants didn't go to movies.

Redford flashed his best Hollywood smile and said, "I gave your lineman my fuel order. May I use your phone?"

"What gas do ya want?" Angel asked in the same husky monotone she used on everyone else.

"Ah, fill both sides," he replied, still smiling. He put his hand on the telephone.

"Jet or gas?" she asked.

"Pardon me?" he said.

"Do ya want avgas or Jet B?" She didn't smile or show any sign of recognizing him.

"Ah, avgas, thanks," the smile was wanning a little.

"One hundred or eighty?" she asked.

"One hundred," he replied.

"How are ya goin' to pay?" Angel inquired bluntly.

"Ah, credit card, if that's all right?" Redford answered, pulling out his wallet. He obviously wanted to use the phone more than he wanted to answer her questions.

"It costs extra," Angel replied. She didn't like to see Derry Air paying banking fees.

"Sure, no problem," he said. "May I use this phone?" he was almost pleading.

"Local call?" she asked.

"No, California. I'll use a calling card," he said.

"Help yourself."

Redford dialed while Angel called the linecrew on the walky-talky that sat crackling on her desk. Redford was forced to shove a finger in his ear to block out her booming radio voice. She confirmed the fuel order with Huey, Duey and Louey. Despite the fact that Redford had spoken to them first, they would not have dared to fill the aircraft until they had received that call.

After a few minutes of conversation on the telephone, Redford had been put on hold. He started to make small talk with Angel.

"Whe're you from?" he asked, breaking back into that million dollar smile again.

"Here," she said.

"Derry?" he asked.

"No, right here," she said, frowning and pointing to the floor.

"You were born on that stool?" he laughed. I thought he was pushing it but Angel stayed calm.

"Almost," she replied, "The airport was built on my parents' farm. I was born in the house down the road."

"Ever get to California?" he asked.

Angel had never travelled further than Tentingtons, the oversize dress shop downtown. "Nope."

"Ever play tennis?"

I doubted Angel "played" anything.

"Horseshoes," she said.

"Pardon me?" Redford asked with another laugh.

"I play horseshoes at the church pit Sunday nights."

"What's horseshoes?" he asked. He was probably wishing he hadn't started this conversation, but he didn't show it.

"We pitch horseshoes onto a metal stake across the yard."

"Is the horse still attached?" Redford laughed but he was watching her to see if he had gone too far.

Angel actually smiled. It was a calendar event. "Nope," was all she said.

Their conversation was interrupted by Huey calling in the fuel total. Redford's party came back on the line. Angel completed his bill, slammed it through the card machine and slapped it on the counter with a pen. Redford signed while cradling the phone and ending his call.

"Thank you very much," he said to Angel, pocketing his bill. "If I come back on Sunday, would you give me a horseshoe lesson?"

"Nope," she replied.

"Well," he said, frowning a little, "maybe I'll see you around."

That was it. Redford left, Angel went back to posting invoices and I sat on the other side of the room with my mouth open. I had just witnessed the most desirable man in the world ask the ugliest woman for a date pitching horseshoes, and get turned down.

Mingy, the owner of Derry Air, came out of his office from behind Angel. "Who was that?" he asked.

Angel looked at the credit card receipt. "Robert Redford," she said, still showing no signs of recognition.

"I've never seen him before." Mingy was obviously as much a movie fan as his receptionist.

"I guess he's just some California cowboy smiling his way

across country on a credit card," Angel replied.

Chapter Ten

Diana

"Lovely Lady in the tower,
What's the runway of the hour?"

The little rhyme was delivered on the control tower frequency by Derry Air customer Bull Muldoone. He was flying his Piper Twin Comanche inbound for a landing. It was one of the many male chauvinistic remarks endured by the only female air traffic controller on the field.

Diana Bates paid dearly for the doubtful privilege of working in an industry dominated by males, but she calmly gave Bull the numbers and asked him to call entering the base leg.

At any given time, the Derry Airport traffic was light. The normal radio transmissions were often separated by silence, except when Diana was working; then the area pilots suddenly became comedians. "Say little lady, do you know what happened to the girl who didn't know the difference between Vaseline and putty?" Bull asked.

You could just imagine him chuckling to the buddies riding with him in the airplane.

There were no air regulations preventing pilots from asking questions on the radio. Diana, on the other hand, worked under a strict manual of operations which left little opportunity for verbal one-upmanship.

She didn't reply. Bull delivered the punch line anyway. "All her windows fell out, hee, hee, hee."

Diana remained silent. When Bull called on the base leg for a landing clearance, she gave it to him in her normal, courteous voice, as if he was a professional airline pilot and not an ignorant amateur.

I met Diana Bates shortly after that incident. She presented herself at the Derry Air front desk to begin flying lessons.

Angel assigned her to me and introduced us. Diana was a tall, pleasant-looking young woman with long, dark hair, a nice smile and a firm handshake. Her steady eyes indicated there was intelligence behind that face.

Diana told me that she wanted to learn to fly, not to penetrate further into a man's world, but to have fun. She had become an air traffic controller because she found aviation interesting and she wanted more. Her quick mind and ATC background made teaching her a pleasure.

Diana's co-workers in the control tower resisted the temptation to treat her differently on the radio, until we started practising takeoffs and landings in the circuit. At Derry Air, the flying instructors had a set of codes pre-arranged with the tower controllers. If we asked for a "touch and go with Alpha," it meant that we wanted the controller to give the student a practise overshoot on the approach, even though there was no conflicting traffic. Since the students didn't know the code, they were not expecting to be told to "pull up and go around". "Bravo on the go," meant we were going to simulate an engine failure after the next takeoff. The code by-passed a lot of explanation and told the controller not to call out the crash truck when he saw the airplane pitch down and head for the ground off the end of the runway.

Diana knew the codes so while she was performing the pre-flight check on the Cherokee one day, I called the tower on our direct line. I explained the situation, and asked the controller to give us an "Alpha" on the third and sixth circuit, and to expect a "Bravo" on the fourth. He agreed.

We got our overshoot on the third approach and we did a simulated engine failure after the fourth takeoff, but after that, we couldn't land. The two guys working the tower took turns telling Diana to "pull up and go around" for no apparent reason on every approach. It was funny at first, but after the third one, the lesson was going into overtime. They were wasting our time and Diana's money.

"Do these guys hate you?" I asked.

"No, they're just having fun. Don't worry, I'll fix them."

On the next downwind leg, she picked up the microphone and said, "Mayday, Mayday, Mayday. Tango Victor Hotel is experiencing a wallet failure and requires an immediate full stop landing."

I couldn't believe it. I had been taught that the sacred international distress call was to be used only in an emergency.

There was a short silence on the radio followed by a chuckle and a clearance to "land immediately on any runway."

"Didn't you just create a lot of paper work for somebody?" I asked Diana.

"Yes," she replied with a smile. "For them."

Chapter Eleven

Doc

Doctor Roy burst into the examining room and stared at me over the top of his glasses. "You're too fat!" he declared immediately. "You call yourself a pilot?" he said, pointing at my round belly with his clipboard. "Look at you! I bet you get sleepy flying above 2,000 feet! Can't you walk past the icebox?"

I couldn't answer. I was in shock. I had never met the man before but in five seconds Doctor Roy had pegged my lifestyle and was giving me a royal dressing down without so much as a "How do you do?"

Doctor Roy was the local Derry physician designated by Transport Canada to give pilot medicals. Angel had given me his phone number when I had asked about renewing my medical.

"Is he any good?" I had asked.

"He delivered me," she said.

It was an interesting endorsement. I had a flash mental picture of a struggling doctor delivering a heavy-duty, baby Angel with a block and tackle. I called and made an appointment.

Doctor Roy's office was in a small, converted house not far from the Derry Airport. I opened the front door to a tiny waiting area. It was packed to standing room only with assorted sick people. Everyone turned and stared at me when I walked in. I picked my way through the crowd to the other end of the room where a short, no-nonsense nurse was busy behind a reception counter. I introduced myself. She gave me a quick nod and a smile, handed me the pilot medical forms on a clipboard and asked me to fill them in.

I found a spot against a wall where I stood and wrote the same answers to the same questions that are on the medical form every year. While I was doing this, an incredible number of patients were being rapidly cycled through several examining rooms. The nurse orchestrated the shuffle while the doctor darted from room to room, his lab coat flowing behind his small, lean body. He appeared to be an older version of the nurse. The office seemed like the right place to come for a quick medical diagnosis and the wrong place for sympathy.

Shortly after I had completed the personal data on the form, the nurse called me to come behind her counter. She checked my weight, vision and vital signs in full view of the waiting room. She asked me many of the questions on the medical that were reserved for the doctor. The whole time she continued answering the phone and juggling the patients. When we were done, she gave me a tiny pill vial to use for a sample. It was obviously designed for low-pressure, accurate plumbing.

"Use the washroom on the other side of the waiting room," she said.

I did and returned through the crowd with my dripping cargo of yellow liquid.

"Leave it on the counter," she said, "and follow me."

She led me into an examining room and asked me to wait for "the Doc".

When he'd burst into the room, I had been trying to find him in the picture of the University of Toronto Graduating Class of 1944 hanging on the wall. I was having trouble, partly because I had never met the man and partly because I needed glasses.

After "the Doc's" initial observation of my size, he checked my form on his clipboard and declared, "You're 10 kilos overweight for your height." He didn't pause long enough for me to counter the declaration. "You have a choice," he said, "either grow taller or lose weight."

"Oh great," I thought to myself, "besides being abrasive, the little old doc thinks he's a comedian."

"Any history of heart problems in your family?" he asked.

"No sir," I replied.

"Well there's going to be if you don't shape up. Keep eating too much and not exercising, and your body is going to explode."

I was admittedly heavy and definitely soft, but the tiny tyrant was bugging me. "I don't think I'm that out-of-shape," I protested.

"Look at you!" he scoffed. "I can't imagine you surviving any kind of airplane crash. The force of all your flab decelerating against a seat belt would cut you in half." He made a scything motion with his clipboard.

"I..." I started to say.

"And if you did survive an accident, I can't see you running away from the burning wreck or carrying any passengers. You'd collapse. How many push-ups can you do? One?"

"I..."

"Come on," he said, dropping to the carpet. "I'll match you."

He proceeded to count off a snappy series of one-armed push-ups, holding his clipboard behind his back. The stethoscope around his neck coiled and uncoiled on the floor as he went up and down.

"Well, maybe I do need some exercise," I admitted. I didn't budge from where I was standing.

He jumped back onto his feet. "Right. Lose 5 kilos before your next medical or I'll flunk you," he said, noting the ultimatum in my file.

I knew I could go to the next town for my next medical, but I still had to get through this one. I didn't say anything.

"Which grad in the photo is me?" he asked.

"Pardon me?" I replied. It took me a second to realize he had flitted on to something else.

"Can you read the fine print below the grad picture?"

I already knew I couldn't. "What's the point?" I asked. I was having trouble keeping up to this peppery old man and I was stalling.

"I've learned two things about pilots your age:" he said, "you've all memorized the eye charts and most of you need glasses. Get an eye exam before your next medical." He noted that comment in my file.

It occurred to me that I might fail this physical and be out of work. I wondered what trick the little tyrant would try next.

"Can you hear this?" he said in a quieter voice.

I couldn't hear anything. "Hear what?" I asked.

He frowned. "Can you hear me asking you if you can hear me?"

"Yes sir," I said quickly.

"Good," he replied loudly.

Then Doctor Roy softened his tone considerably and asked me a series of questions that were not on the medical form. "Are your parents still alive? Brothers? Sisters? Are you married? How much alcohol do you drink in a week? Have you travelled off the continent lately? When did you last visit a dentist?"

I gave him answers I thought he wanted to hear. After each one, I expected a lecture, but "the Doc" just made notes without commenting. He continued the questions as if he was genuinely interested in my well-being. After five minutes, I realized he had built an accurate profile of my family and my living habits. I started to relax.

"That's it then," he said abruptly. "You'll be okay for another year if you work on that weight and get your eyes examined." He signed my Licence Renewal Certificate and handed it to me with a quick smile.

I was thinking that maybe Doctor Roy wasn't that bad after all. As he turned to go I said, "I'm not going to lose weight instructing in airplanes all day. Do you have any suggestions?"

"Sure," he said quickly, "I can break both your arms or wire your jaw shut." He burst out laughing at his own joke. "But either way you wouldn't be able to work. See Barb and ask her for a 1,500-calorie diet and a 10BX exercise book. I'll see you in five kilos."

I started to say "thanks", but he was gone.

Chapter Twelve

Tiger by the tail

Instructor friend Henry Rains agreed to fly with me for instrument and multi-engine training. We started in a Cherokee 140 after I completed the simulator work with Dutch. The idea was to practise in the slower and cheaper single-engine airplane first. I thought it was a waste of time.

"Henry," I said, while flying with a hood over my eyes to limit outward vision, "I could do this with my eyes closed. We should be in the Twin Comanche now."

"Trust me," he replied from the right seat, "you need this training. The twin is a whole new ball game. I know."

Henry "knew" because he had recently completed his own multi-engine IFR training. He had offered to instruct me at no cost because it helped him build his own multi-engine hours. We were taking advantage of a loophole in the government rules. Instructors were required to have at least 50 hours on multi-engine airplanes before they could teach multi-engine flying but there was nothing that said they could not teach instrument flying on multi-engine aircraft. We didn't try to understand the loophole, we just took advantage of it.

Henry switched me to the Twin Comanche after four hours in the Cherokee. It was a hot airplane to any pilot who had only flown single-engine trainers. Each of its two engines were more powerful than the one in the Cherokee, but the cabin was the same size. It could hit 200 mph in level flight.

At Henry's suggestion, I sat in the Twin Comanche to familiarize myself whenever I had a few spare minutes. I ran through the normal procedures and the emergency drills in the Pilot Operating Handbook. When the time came for my first lesson, I believed I knew everything.

The only time Mingy would let staff fly the airplane was after hours. I was still doing early morning flying lessons with Dutch toward his Commercial Pilot Licence. They were long days.

51

My first flight in the twin was to be an introduction to the airplane on a local flight followed by a simple holding procedure under the hood and an approach to the airport for a couple of practise touch-and-go landings. I climbed into the airplane, buckled up, strapped a clipboard to my leg and started down the checklist. Henry settled into the right seat. I fired up the engines one at a time and taxied to the runway. The air traffic controller cleared us to go. I lined up with the centreline. I knew what to do. The Pilot Handbook had told me: smoothly apply full power, raise the nose at 85 mph, liftoff at 90, climb at 120, raise the landing gear when there is no longer sufficient runway remaining on which to land and reduce the power to 25 inches of manifold pressure and 2500 rpm using the throttles first and then the propeller pitch.

I pushed the twin throttles smoothly to the stops. It was exciting. I had never been pressed into my seat by acceleration before. It was a rush. The lift-off speed came quickly and I missed it. I was too busy grinning.

"Raise the nose," Henry yelled over the full power snarl of the two engines.

I pulled back, but the controls on the Twin Comanche were heavier than I had experienced. The airplane stayed on the runway, galloping along on its nose wheel at 100 mph.

"Nose up," Henry prompted.

I pulled harder. The nosed pitched up and we were airborne. The nose continued to pitch up. The airplane was now obeying all of my previous inputs. We were headed skyward with no view forward. The airspeed began to drop as the climb steepened.

"Lower the nose," Henry yelled, "airspeed 120."

I relaxed my back pressure on the control wheel.

"Raise the gear," Henry yelled.

I looked down to find the landing gear handle and pulled it up. The retracting wheels changed the airplane's balance. It started into a shallow dive from 500 feet with the engines at full power.

"Raise the nose," Henry said, "airspeed 120, reduce the power."

Henry spoke loudly but calmly as my well-rehearsed first takeoff went to hell in a high speed hand basket.

I was proving once again that nothing replaces actual experience. I was embarrassed. I thought the wild gyrations were reserved for student pilots, not experienced flying instructors. I reduced my control inputs and the oscillations diminished. I looked down to set the throttles to 25 inches on the manifold pressure gauge. The airplane slipped into another dive.

"Pull the throttles back to where you think they should be without looking and then check the needles," Henry said. "Try it with the rpm."

I reached for the propeller controls while hauling the Twin Comanche out of the dive. I pulled the prop levers too hard. The engines groaned as the propeller governors fought to cut the rpm in half while the throttles were at high power. I pushed the prop levers back up. The engines surged ahead.

"I'll get it," Henry yelled. I could feel his hand over mine on the pitch controls. "We don't want to break anything. Turn left to 120 degrees."

I rolled the airplane left. The response was good, but the mass of the engines and fuel in the wings caused me to over control again. We were headed for a spiral dive. I pulled back, the dive tightened. I reduced the bank angle and the Twin Comanche headed skyward at a great rate and a declining speed.

"Airspeed 120," Henry called out. I thought I could hear a knowing smile in his voice but I didn't have time to look.

And so it went. I successfully over controlled the airplane in all phases of flight. Henry showed no mercy. Whenever I was close to mastering a maneuver, he gave me something else to do. We covered various climbs, descents and turns, slow flight and stalls. Then Henry asked me to set up the airplane like I was going to approach for a landing with the gear and flaps down and the power back but staying at 4,000 feet. I did as he said.

"Now show me an overshoot procedure," Henry said.

I pushed the throttles up. The airplane accelerated smartly. I reached for the flap lever and Henry pulled the power back on the right engine.

"You have a simulated engine failure," he said calmly. "The runway is behind you and the ground is at 4,000 feet."

The airplane was at 4,400 feet but was starting to lose altitude. I raised the nose and retracted the flaps. We were still going down and the airplane had started rolling to the right from the thrust of the left engine. I corrected with left rudder and aileron. The propeller on the idling right engine was dragging us down.

"When you complete the emergency check and are ready to feather the propeller," Henry said, "I'll simulate it with zero thrust throttle on the dead engine."

I pulled the landing gear lever up. The "gear up" horn started blaring. I had 200 feet of altitude remaining above 4,000 feet and we were still rolling right. I pushed full left rudder and called out, "Mixture, pitch, power, gear up, flaps up, dead foot — dead engine; the right engine is dead."

"You're dead," Henry interrupted. He pointed at the airspeed. I had let it drop below the minimum speed needed to maintain control of the airplane. We were rolling into the theoretical ground at 4,000 feet and there was nothing I could do to prevent it. It was the most basic but deadliest mistake a multi-engine pilot could make.

"We'll do it again when you least expect it," Henry replied. He reapplied the right engine power with one hand and handed me the hood with the other. "Put this on. You're cleared direct to the Derry NDB to hold southwest, maintain 3,000 feet."

"Okay slave driver," I replied.

"Okay, nothing. That was an IFR clearance and I'm waiting for your readback."

I had to adjust to flying by the instruments, set up a descent to 3,000 feet, tune in the Derry NDB on the ADF and read back the holding clearance all at the same time. It wasn't pretty, but I did it. Then I turned the airplane toward the signal according to the ADF needle. The heading was 330 degrees. I leveled off at 3,000 feet while figuring out how I was going to enter the hold from the inbound track. The ADF needle swung from ahead to behind. My inconsiderate instructor must have given me the exercise when we were nearly over the transmitter.

"Time flies at 170 mph," Henry said. "You could have slowed down as soon as you received the holding clearance, as long as you let ATC know. If you haven't figured out the hold entry procedure, just turn to the outbound track and go from there."

"Is it hot in here?" I asked.

"Not for me," Henry replied.

I turned outbound. After once around the holding pattern, Henry cleared me for a simulated NDB instrument approach to Runway 06 at the Derry airport. With the Twin Comanche slowed down to near Cherokee speeds, I found I could almost keep up to the airplane. When I finished the approach, the airport was in front of us.

"Take the hood off," Henry said. The active runway is 24. Break off to the right for a circling approach. You're number two. We'll do a stop-and-go landing and takeoff followed by one circuit."

"Okay."

"This airplane sits low to the ground so you'll tend to flare out too high," Henry said. "This wouldn't be a problem except the up elevator control runs out just when you need a bit more to cushion the drop."

I recognized the comments as a warning that this was my opportunity to demonstrate that I was no better than all the other rookie Twin Comanche pilots who screwed up their first landing. My only defence was that recognition and reaction are two things that are far apart when you're tired.

"You're cleared for a stop-and-go," Henry said.

I turned the airplane onto final and lined it up with the runway. Over the numbers, I cut the power and flared out. We were too high. The airplane continued to drop. I pulled back on the control wheel but it wouldn't budge. The elevators were already all the way up. We hit with a thud.

"Come to a complete stop," Henry said. "That will give you a better chance to keep up with the airplane on the takeoff."

When I was ready to go, I applied full power. By paying less attention to the exhilaration and more to the acceleration, I minimized the gyrations after the takeoff.

"Do one circuit for a full stop landing," Henry said.

On the downwind leg, I was able to relax a bit and enjoy flying this thoroughbred airplane. The Twin Comanche responded smartly to control inputs and power changes even with the drag of the landing gear and flaps.

Henry reached under my hand and pulled back the power on the right engine.

"Simulated engine failure," he said.

I reacted immediately. I was determined to identify and feather the dead engine without losing altitude. With one eye on the airspeed and the other on the horizon, I called out the engine failure emergency procedure. "Mixture, pitch, power, flaps up ..."

"No! No! No!" Henry yelled over top of my chant. He was holding my right hand so I couldn't do anything. "Use your head before your hands." He pointed out my side of the airplane with his other hand. "There is a runway right down there. Forget the dead engine and land the airplane."

After we touched down and taxied to the ramp, I said, "Does this mean I have to go back to flying instruments on the Cherokee?"

"Hell, no," Henry replied. "I'm having more fun watching

DERRY AIR

you wrestle this thing."

Chapter Thirteen

April fool

Derry Air had competition on the airport. Condor Aviation also offered flying training, charter flights, aircraft maintenance, hangar storage, fuel, aircraft sales and sightseeing flights. The natural rivalry between the two companies was spirited but friendly. If Condor needed a tire for an aircraft, the Derry Air staff would happily loan one and then tell everybody that the wheels were falling off the aircraft next door.

This good-natured competition was taken to a new level when the Derry linecrew, Huey, Duey and Louey, worked the late shift on March 31st. They waited until everyone else on the airport had gone home and then modified the huge sign on Condor's hangar to read, "CONDOM AVIATION."

The altered name was on the airside of the hangar so the staff arriving at the airport the next morning couldn't see it. Neither could the controllers in the tower, but to the pilots and passengers of the early morning commuter flights, it was in plain view.

The captain of a Boeing 737 taxiing past Condor made the first comment on the ground frequency, "Looks like a safe place to fly," he said.

Diana Bates was the controller. "Say again?" she asked.

"That school looks like a 'safe' place to learn how to fly."

"Sure," Diana replied. She had no idea.

This encouraged a pilot on an arriving corporate Saberliner to join in. "It must be an 'up and coming' flying school," he said.

Before Diana could answer, the 737 captain shot back, "I bet they specialize in night flying!"

"Or precautionary approaches," the Saberliner pilot countered, "with lots of touch and goes."

"What are you guys talking about?" Diana asked.

The two pilots ignored her. They were having too much fun.

"I wonder if they teach short and soft landings?" the corporate pilot asked.

"I wonder if they have a simulator?" the 737 captain said with a snort.

Just then a Beechcraft King Air from the United States landed. A female voice with a southern drawl checked in on the frequency. "Derry Ground, one zero alpha, taxi to the ramp."

"One zero alpha is cleared to the ramp."

"One zero alpha, roger. Say, that's quite a combination y'all got here, Condom Aviation and Derry Air. Does one teach front course and the other teach back course approaches?"

"It's Condor Aviation," Diana replied.

"Not on my side it's not," the female pilot said. "It's definitely Condom Aviation."

Several of us at Derry Air heard the exchange on the office monitor. We walked out onto the ramp to have a look. Sure enough, the big raised letter 'r' on the side of Condor's old World War II hangar had an extension. Two sheets of plywood had been added in a poorly-matched blue colour. The sloppy, homemade alteration certainly looked like the work of Huey, Duey and Louey.

News of the prank swept across the airport. The irate manager at Condor called Derry Air's owner Irving Mingy. He demanded the immediate removal of the plywood.

"What makes you think we put it up there?" Mingy asked calmly. It was one of the few times I had seen him smile.

"Because you have the only de-icing truck with a boom long enough to reach the sign."

"I'll look into it," Mingy replied.

He waited until Huey, Duey and Louey arrived for their afternoon shift. He waited too long. Someone phoned the *Derry Daily*, the local newspaper. A photographer was dispatched before the sign was fixed. A picture of "CONDOM AVIATION" appeared the next day on the front page of the regional news section.

Condor's manager was furious. He called Mingy again and tried to tear a strip off him, but Mingy just laughed it off.

"You ought to put a sock on that temper of yours," Mingy said. "It's no big deal."

He was wrong. The newspaper photo was a big deal. It turned into the kind of advertising that money couldn't buy. That weekend, people who previously didn't know Derry had an airport, drove out to see the sign. Condor's manager capitalized on the activity and ran a special on sightseeing flights that kept two of their Cessna 172s busy both Saturday and Sunday. The picture prompted people who had been thinking about taking flying lessons to visit Condor for an introductory flight. Even some of Derry's flying school customers were drawn across the ramp by curiosity.

On Monday, Condor's manager had his linecrew paint a sheet of plywood and lean it against his hangar facing Derry Air. It read, "Condor 1, Derry 0."

Chapter Fourteen

Highway patrol

The police contracted Derry Air to supply an aircraft and pilot for airborne patrol of the area highways during the summer. The flying school provided a Cessna 172 that was rigged with an extra antenna for the police radio and a huge "POLICE" decal on the fuselage.

Derry Air chief instructor Eric Daedalus usually took the flights. He had discovered that his constant sense of humour was matched by the police officer assigned to the aircraft, Corporal Roger Shirley. The two jokesters made a good pair. Roger would often "chase" Eric to the airport with the cruiser lights flashing and siren screaming. In the air, the pilot would get even by shoving forward on the control wheel and pinning the officer to the ceiling whenever he loosened his seatbelt.

The purpose of the patrol flights was to monitor traffic from the air and issue tickets to violators, mainly speeders, via an officer and a car on the ground. Different sections of highway in the area with pavement markings were designated for each patrol. Eric flew from the left front seat and Corporal Shirley rode behind him. Both men watched the same section of highway for speeding vehicles. When they spotted a hot prospect, Roger timed it between the pavement markers. He then radioed the violation to the officer on the ground parked on the side of the road. That policeman waved the motorist over and issued the citation. In between "hits" there would be jokes passed over the intercom and the police radio. Eric and Roger became well known on the police network.

Eric told me about one speeder who illustrated the advantage of using the aircraft. "I spotted a motorcycle weaving in and out of traffic. The biker looked like the two per cent who give the other 98 per cent a bad name. When he couldn't pass cars, he went between them.

"'You might want to see this one,' I said to Shirley.

He looked over my shoulder. 'Oh yah, road trash,' he said.

"I turned and followed the guy. Roger called out the violations to the cop who was standing beside his cruiser. He pointed a finger at the chopper driver as he approached and hooked his thumb toward the side of the road. The biker looked at the cop, assessed the situation for a second and decided he could beat the rap. He gave the cop a one-fingered salute, cranked his throttle and shot between the next two cars. He continued to bob, weave and squirt through the traffic. The policeman continued to lean against his car to give the suspect the impression that he was making an easy get-away. I applied power.

"The biker kept his speed up all the way to the first exit at Derry. I had trouble staying with him in the Cessna. A few times he pulled away from us when we were doing 100 knots. Roger continued adding to a growing list of charges. Once the rider was off the highway, he slowed down. He cruised through a few stop signs and eventually pulled into a driveway and parked the hog behind the house.

"I circled while Roger vectored the cop to the location. He parked in the driveway, checked the motorcycle and banged on the back door. The dumb biker answered the knock. The cop handcuffed him and led him to the cruiser. On the way, Roger read him the charges over the other cop's portable radio. The guy looked up. From 1,500 feet, I could tell what he said. So could Roger.

"'Save it for the judge,' Roger replied."

Chapter Fifteen

Bake day

When I started instructing at Derry Air, Henry told me that Orville Kenny's landing strip was the best place to teach off-airport approaches and grass field landings and takeoffs. He showed me where it was on a map.

"Go on Saturdays," he said.

"Why Saturday?"

"You'll see."

I booked an off-airport lesson to the Kenny's strip with Melville Passmore for the following Saturday. The pudgy farm boy's face lit up when I told him.

"That's my most favorite place," he said.

On Saturday I briefed Melville on what we were going to do: low level navigation to the field followed by an off-airport approach and a grass field landing. In the airplane, Melville asked for taxi instructions for "a local flight east".

The ground controller said, "Another run to the Kenny's?"

"Affirmative," Melville shouted into the microphone.

The flight was an ideal lesson. The Kenny's strip was about 25 nautical miles from Derry across farmland and little else. It provided Melville with a good map reading workout. He successfully followed our path along his chart to what appeared to be a well-groomed landing strip. I couldn't believe it. There were three familiar airplanes on the ground and two in the air. They were training aircraft from the two flying schools at Derry.

I had Melville join the traffic pattern and set up for a low and over to inspect the field. It was a good coordination exercise. He had to fly at minimum speed, low to the ground, in level flight, while looking down at the strip. He managed three out of four. He slowed down, extended the flaps, descended to treetop level and looked at the field. He didn't hold the altitude. We flew the length of the strip descending until we were almost touching down. The trees at the far end loomed ahead of us.

Before it was too late, I tapped him on the shoulder. "Getting a close look, Melville?"

"Yup," he said, and then looked forward. "Oh my gosh!"

He added full power. We cleared the trees and circled around for a landing. Melville approached at minimum speed with full flap and planted the Cherokee on the first part of the strip. The grass was smooth and hard. Melville retracted the flaps and stopped the airplane before we had used up half of the 2,500 feet.

Melville shut the engine down and we both climbed out. There was an older man in farmer coveralls standing and talking to an instructor and student from Condor on the grass parking area near the house. I introduced myself as a new instructor from Derry Air.

"Pleased to meet you," the older man said and then laughed. He seemed like a kindly fellow. His handshake came with a wide palm and rough skin. The tanned and leathery face was well creased with smile lines. "I'm Orville Kenny," he said and then laughed some more. "I've seen this fella before," he added, nodding to Melville. "You're the Passmore boy, right?"

"Yes sir," Melville replied, but he was looking toward the house. "How's the missus?"

"She's fine, fine," Orville said with another laugh. "You'd better scoot in and say 'Hello' to her."

Melville headed toward the house as fast as his farmer legs would take him without actually running. He didn't wait or look back to see if I was following.

Orville answered the puzzled look on my face. "The missus bakes on Saturday mornings."

The thought of farm baked goodies made my mouth water but I didn't think it would look good if I ran after Melville to the kitchen of a woman I had never met, expecting her to serve me breakfast. I stood by Orville and watched the Condor Cessna 150 being started and taxied to the side of the runway.

"Your wife must be a good cook," I said, pointing to the visiting airplanes.

Orville patted his stomach and laughed, "I think you would be safe to say that." I was hoping he would invite me inside, but he continued to watch the Condor airplane. The student pilot was doing his pre-takeoff checks.

"Your strip is as smooth as asphalt," I said, thinking that the compliment might help get me in the house.

Orville's natural smile widened. "I try to keep it in good shape," he said and then laughed. Apparently most of Orville's sentences were accompanied with a chuckle.

"When I'm mowing it," he added, "I roller it too."

We watched the Cessna takeoff.

"I'll show you the rig," Orville said.

He led the way to a long machine shed covered with galvanized steel. My comment must have led him to believe that I was more interested in his lawn mower than his wife's baking. He was wrong but I didn't say anything. When we were passing behind the house, I could smell good things coming from the kitchen. Orville swung open a broad door at one end of the shed to reveal a monstrous red tractor. It was gleaming. There was a twelve unit gang mower hooked on behind with the outer reels folded up, also gleaming. Behind that was what looked like an ancient metal roller. It stood about three metres high and looked like it might have originally been pulled by a team of horses. There were other, equally large, four-wheel drive tractors and various pieces of equipment in the shed that indicated that Orville was a cash crop farmer, a very successful cash crop farmer.

"Where is your airplane?" I asked.

Orville blushed a little and kicked some dirt on the shed floor. "I don't have an airplane."

"Do you fly?"

"Nope."

"So the landing strip is a hobby for you?" I asked.

"You might say that. I like airplanes and people. Having the runway brings both."

"Did you ever think about learning to fly?"

"Oh, you can't teach old dogs new tricks," he said and laughed.

"Well, that's the thing about flying," I said. "There's no trick to it. Have you ever been up in one of these airplanes?"

"Oh sure," he said. "The boys have had me up a couple of times. We took a picture of the place from the air. That was fun, but actually flying the airplane is another kettle of fish."

To me, Orville's runway was a big sign from a shy but friendly country boy that he wanted to be involved in aviation. There was no other explanation as to why he would have dedicated 2,500 feet of prime farmland to a 50-foot wide strip of grass just for the use of the Derry Air instructors.

"Well, if you're interested, you might want to try a lesson."

"Oh, us farm boys are kind of thick in the head."

"I know. I teach the Passmore boy, remember?" Orville blushed at the forward manner of my city-boy talk.

"If you can operate all that machinery," I continued, "I'd think you'd find flying pretty easy. Melville does."

He drew some lines in the shed's dirt floor with the toe of his boot. "Well, the missus has been saying I should try it."

I had been right. Orville did want to fly.

"I've got a half hour," I said, kissing my thoughts of fresh baked pie goodbye. "I'll give you a brief lesson right now."

He smiled but still didn't move. It was like he was afraid of shattering a life-long dream.

"Come on. There'll be no obligation to continue. If I can't teach you, I won't tell anyone if you don't, but I'll eat my hat."

"Okay, sonny, but remember, you talked yourself into it."

I didn't take the time to brief him or to do a walkaround. We just climbed into the airplane and took off. In the air, I had Orville try straight and level flight and a few turns. He was a natural. His grin got wider and his smile lines grew deeper. The only problem was our lack of time. He was just getting started when I told him that we had to head back.

On the ground, he shook my hand long and hard. "Sonny, you got yourself an old dog student as long as you'll have me."

"Great!"

Henry came from the direction of the house with a student. "Been doing a little sightseeing, Orville?" he asked.

"Yup," was all the older man said but he was grinning hard.

"Well, we'll be off," Henry said. "Take care."

"Yup."

When Henry had climbed into the Cherokee with his student, Orville said, "Come on in and meet the missus."

Annabelle Kenny looked like a typical farm wife. She was round, big bosomed and rosy cheeked. Her hair was tied back in a bun. A full length apron covered a cotton print dress.

When Orville introduced us, he said, "Annabelle, I want you to meet my flying instructor."

The wording was not lost on her.

"I saw you two going up from the kitchen window. If you've talked this silly old man into lessons, I thank you indeed. I don't know how you did it. I've tried for thirty years without success."

"He's going to make a good student," I replied.

Melville was sitting at the kitchen table eating what was probably his third piece of pie. There were buns, muffins and butter tarts heaped on a serving dish on the table. My mouth started to water just looking at them but I was going to be late for my next booking.

"Come on, Melville," I said. "We have to get that airplane back to Derry Air while we can still get it off the ground. Mrs. Kenny, I'll be calling your husband about his next lesson when I get back to the office."

"The name's Annabelle," she said while wrapping two butter tarts in a napkin. "Here's a reminder."

"Thanks."

Chapter Sixteen

Wallflower of Death

Irving Mingy said anyone could learn to fly. This was the flying school owner's response to staff suggestions that certain student pilots would be better off learning basket weaving. He could say that because he didn't have to fly with them.

I did. That's how I met Helga Beauregart.

That day started with Derry Air chief instructor Eric Daedalus saying, "I see you're booked with the Wallflower of Death." He laughed, but then his tone turned serious when he added, "Don't expect much from her; expect a lot from yourself."

"What do you mean by that?" I asked.

"Check her file and if you have any questions, ask any instructor here."

Helga's folder indicated she was a female teenager with too many flying hours for someone who had never soloed. The other instructors had covered every lesson on the course several times. None had indicated any progress. Short comments like "uninterested," "absent-minded," and "hopeless" filled the file.

Before I started working at Derry Air, Helga's father had brought her in and announced she would learn to fly. Helga was proving him wrong. The file comments confirmed it, but Mingy agreed with the dad as long as he continued to pay. The instructors' solution was to pass the fledging kamikaze on to someone else.

When I met Helga, my first impression was to doubt her gender. She was gangly and looked the same coming or going. A bad case of acne had erased most indications of her age. She wore baggy jeans and a wrinkled T-shirt. Her most outstanding feature was a scabby rash covering her bare arms and hands.

Angel introduced us. I instinctively thrust my hands into my pockets.

"Pleased to meet you," she said shyly.

I must have stared at her arms too long. "I got into some poison ivy while picking wild raspberries," she said, giving her right arm a good scratch and topping a couple of scabs.

I had decided before meeting Helga, that we would do soft field landings and takeoffs at the Kenny's grass strip. Her log book showed many repeated hours of practise at the airport. I theorized that the soft field work would give her a change of scenery. I gave Helga a pre-flight briefing on landing and taking off from a grass field with obstacles. She listened and answered my questions correctly, but she didn't seem very interested. I spent the whole time wishing she would stop picking her arms.

It was warm outside but in self-defense I wore a jacket to cover my skin. I started off by demonstrating a soft field takeoff and landing at the Derry Airport. I had Helga try the same thing. Her performance wasn't bad for someone who hadn't soloed. We headed for the Kenny's grass strip. I flew the first sequence. For the approach, I extended full flaps on the Cherokee, slowed the airplane to a crawl, reduced the power and dove for the field. The biggest danger in this maneuver was allowing the airspeed to drop too far. The Cherokee had a laminar wing flow which worked well as long as it had sufficient airspeed.

I timed the descent so we skimmed over the hydro wires that ran in front of the strip's northern boundary. At the last second, I hauled back on the control wheel and held the aircraft just off the ground until it stalled onto the grass.

I had talked the whole way in, describing the technique. As I taxied back for the takeoff, I asked Helga if she had any questions. She smiled nervously and said, "No." She seemed more interested in the wild flowers in the grass.

I demonstrated the takeoff. On the grass, the Cherokee accelerated slowly, but I held the right amount of control wheel back pressure and milked the airplane into the air in time to clear the trees at the other end.

During the climbout, I gave Helga control. "Okay, now you try it," I said.

She grasped the control wheel and the throttle with her scabby hands. For the approach, she reduced the power, extended the flaps and set up the minimum speed the way I had shown her. As we neared the wires, she raised the nose of the aircraft to clear the obstacles. It was the classical wrong thing to do. The speed dropped.

"Lower the nose and add power Helga," I demanded clearly.

The space remaining and the sluggishness of the airplane at low speed left little time for the correct response. Helga did nothing.

"More power!" I yelled. We were losing speed and altitude. It would be a toss up whether we would hit the wires or stall out first. At this point of any lesson, the instructor normally takes control. I already had my hand on the control wheel on my side. I looked at Helga's rashed mitt gripping the throttle. I turned to scream the instructions that would save us straight into her ear but Helga's head was turned. She was looking out the side window at something on the ground.

The number of things that flash through your mind in a crisis is amazing. I remember weighing the relative consequences of either grabbing the throttle, poison ivy and all, or flying the powerless airplane under the wires and leaving its wheels on the fence. The choices were: save the airplane and lose the hand to disease or save the hand and chance the crash and Mingy's wrath.

It was easier to do nothing and crash, but at the last possible second I shot my left arm up into my jacket sleeve and used it to shove the hand-covered throttle into the instrument panel. The little engine roared. I was able to milk the staggering Cherokee over the wires.

I didn't try to land. We flew across the field, trading time for airspeed. I glanced at Helga. She was still looking out her side window. I retracted the flaps and headed toward the airport. I had survived that one, but I knew I would spend the next three weeks looking at my left hand.

"What did you see Helga?" I asked sarcastically.

She turned and smiled cheerfully, "It looked like there were wild raspberries along the fence."

69

Chapter Seventeen

Sunshine Superman

"I've been promoted," Susan said. I was walking into the house late one evening. I had finished a day at Derry Air with another lesson in the Twin Comanche with Henry.

"That's great honey," I replied. I was tired but injected as much enthusiasm as I could muster. "Tell me about it."

"I start as assistant manager at the Lookout Ridge store on the other side of town next week."

"Good for you," I said. "Does this mean no more macaroni and cheese?"

"Six times a week instead of seven," she said with a laugh. "I'll be making more money."

Susan's announcement didn't surprise me. She had worked her way up to a buyer's job in the retail fashion industry before we were married. I knew that her present sales clerk position was just to get her foot in the door with a new employer. Susan had a special talent for retailing. She had a way of drawing the most out of people without offending them. I knew if the management at the Fashion and Design Emporium were sharp, they'd recognize her abilities.

I did. Susan had been applying her organizing technique to me at home. In my meagre time off since we had moved into Windy Acres, I had rigged a stall in the barn for her horse, fixed the water pump, put up hay and strung an electric wire around the pasture to compensate for the poor condition of the existing fence. These were no small feats for a city boy whose mechanical skills were previously untested and whose knowledge of farming was restricted to the fact that chocolate milk did not come from brown cows.

"I think you should get a horse," Susan said.

This came flat out. There had been no previous discussion about me and a horse. The announcement got my attention.

"Tell me why I want a horse?"

"Well, if you had a horse, we could go riding together and when you're not riding him, he could be company for Cricket.

Horses get lonely, you know, and two horses are nearly as cheap to keep as one."

The reference to "he" indicated there was already a candidate for this new horse position.

"What's his name?"

She blushed. She loved steering people but she didn't like getting caught doing it. She put her arms around me.

"Sunny. A girl at the stables near Derry used him for show jump-ing but he's getting old. She's looking for a good home to retire him from jumping. He's big and gentle. He's perfect for you."

"We both know how much I would use a horse even if he was perfect. Are you going to tell me the real reason why we should be doing this?"

Susan blushed some more. "I want to teach riding here but I can't put novice riders on Cricket."

I liked that idea immediately. Giving riding lessons would keep Susan busy while I worked late and it would put her in touch with other people interested in horses.

"How much might a good home expect to pay for Sunny?"

Susan the sales girl knew that a buyer asking the price was hooked. She got all excited and gave me a big hug. "He's only $500. The owner will let me pay for him in installments out of my new salary. We'll fix up a stall next to Cricket in the barn and I've arranged for one of the neighbours to help you build a riding corral."

"I think it's a great idea."

"Yahoo! You'll really like him. He's slow and plodding, just like you!"

Sunny came to Windy Acres at the end of the month. The name was short for Sunshine Superman and he was huge. In horse parlance, he stood 17 hands. That equates to two metres tall to the shoulder. Sunny's breeding was half workhorse and half thoroughbred. The combination created a gentle giant who supposedly could leap tall buildings in a single bound.

I was home when Sunny was delivered. It was a toss-up who was more excited, Susan or Cricket. Susan's mare danced around and squealed on the other side of the fence while Sunny was being backed off the horse trailer. Susan cried. The second most important day in a girl's life is when she gets her second horse.

Susan led Sunny into the corral while I held the gate. Cricket pranced up to him. They exchanged sniffs. Then Cricket turned around, lifted her tail and presented her butt to Sunny's face.

Unfortunately he was a gelding, so he wasn't interested in that end. Cricket backed into him but there was nothing he could do for her. When she realized that her new stable mate wasn't going to make a woman out of her, Cricket shifted her weight onto her front legs and kicked him in the chest with both back feet.

Susan was upset. "Cricket, you should be ashamed of yourself!" she yelled after the retreating mare.

Sunny took it in stride. He had obviously been exposed to hussy horses before. It was obvious who would be wearing the horse pants in the horse side of the family, but he didn't seem to mind.

Chapter Eighteen

Pineapple

The Derry Air office was in an uproar. Bull Muldoone had arrived to go flying with two friends. Muldoone was large, loud and ignorant. The spoiled, middle-aged owner of a local construction company kept a Piper Twin Comanche in the Derry Air hangar and he wanted it out — now.

I walked into the office from a lesson with a student pilot to witness Muldoone chewing out Derry Air owner Irving Mingy. It was something I had never seen before and would not have advised.

"I just saw my airplane," Muldoone bellowed. "Those airhead lineboys of yours stuck it in the back of the hangar again and covered it with dirt." He punctuated his complaint with stabs of a cigar butt close to Mingy's face. "I'm tired of this second-rate operation," Muldoone continued, "and when I get my airplane out, I might not come back." During his tirade, Muldoone made sure that the construction buddies who had come with him were taking full notice of his demonstration.

Mingy didn't flinch. I waited for the explosion. I thought the ex-paratrooper would send Muldoone packing with his Twin Comanche sticking out of his pants. I underestimated Mingy's capacity to curb his wrath when business income was at stake.

"I'm sorry you didn't call ahead and give us a chance to clean the airplane and pull it out for you," Mingy said quietly but firmly. "Have a coffee and we'll do it right away."

The words and the set of his crooked jaw were well chosen. Muldoone was ready to roar again, but was stopped by a flicker of recognition that possibly he was addressing something more powerful than he realized. He ungraciously accepted the apology. "We can wait a couple of minutes, but make it quick."

The confrontation was a product of Muldoone's past handling of the Derry Air linecrew. He treated them like scum, haranguing them every time he came to the airport, if only to hear his voice echo off the hangar walls. Huey, Duey and Louey rose to the occasion, ensuring they were never yelled at for nothing. They always parked Muldoone's airplane in the back of the hangar under the birds' favourite beam. Whenever they saw his orange and red 4X4 pull into the parking lot, they took a coffee break at the terminal building and turned off their radio. This was what they were doing now.

Angel phoned the terminal to roust them while Mingy recruited the mechanics from the Derry Air maintenance shop to pull out the Twin Comanche. Muldoone poured himself a coffee and plopped down in the lounge area of the flying school. He sat with his construction boots on the table and held court with his two friends.

I finished with my student and went to the hangar to help. We moved about eight airplanes to get the Twin Comanche out. By the time we pulled it onto the ramp, Huey, Duey and Louey arrived and hosed the worst of the bird dirt off. Huey then gassed the airplane while Duey and Louey cleaned the windows with used hand towels from the metal shop.

I was helping Darcy Philips, Derry Air's chief mechanic, push the other aircraft back into the hangar when Mingy came out of the office and asked him to add air to the Twin Comanche's sagging tires.

"Okay, and I'll have the power cart and the fire extinguisher ready," Darcy said. Apparently Muldoone rarely flew and was a menace when he did. I hung around to watch.

The customer-from-hell emerged with his buddies when Darcy was finishing with the tires. "Hurry up, you ramp rat," Muldoone roared at the mechanic. Then he climbed into the airplane. He didn't say "thank you" and didn't do a walkaround inspection. For all he knew, Huey had filled the gas tanks with water, a possibility that had crossed my mind.

The Twin Comanche is a sleek thoroughbred of an airplane. Seeing Muldoone and his equally fat friends squeeze into it was like watching old wrestlers donning tights.

"Pineapple," Darcy muttered under his breath as he walked by me coiling the air hose.

"What did you call him?" I asked.

"The man's a pineapple," he said. "Talking to Muldoone is like climbing a cactus in a bathing suit."

The need for the power cart was soon obvious. The battery was low from sitting and Muldoone soon flattened it completely. He stuck his fat lips through the small pilot-side window and roared at Darcy to plug him in. Darcy was already wheeling the power cart toward the airplane.

Once he was energized, Muldoone held one finger on the electric primer and another on the starter. His other hand pumped the throttle. The engine coughed, caught and revved to nearly full power. The brakes were on but the sudden asymmetric thrust jerked the airplane to one side. Darcy was ready and jumped clear, taking the power cable with him. As soon as the other engine started, Muldoone roared away leaving two pools of avgas soaking the ramp.

"I'd be happy if he didn't come back," Darcy said.

It was wishful thinking. As soon as we had put the power cart away, we could hear the Twin Comanche returning from well down the taxiway. The engines sounded like two meat grinders full of spoons. Both cowlings were blowing oil.

Muldoone shut the airplane down and wriggled out. "Hey grease monkey," he yelled at Darcy, "fix this piece of junk." Then to his passengers he said, "Come on, let's find some beers."

Darcy told me later that Muldoone had opened the manually controlled wastegates on the turbocharged engines all the way. The result was an extra 100 horsepower courtesy of intake boost pressure intended only for the thin air above 15,000 feet. The engines held together for the length of the runway before the cylinder head bolts stretched to relieve the pressure. Muldoone had managed to fly one "watch-this-guys" takeoff, do a tight circuit and land. The engine rattlings we heard were the cylinder heads slamming up and down on the stretched bolts with each stroke of the pistons.

"That one cowboy takeoff probably cost the stupid pineapple $25,000 in repairs," Darcy said.

I happened to be walking past the linecrew office when Mingy was lecturing Huey, Duey and Louey about disappearing on Muldoone.

"Your unscheduled coffee break this morning nearly cost us the loss of $25,000 in repair work. Fortunately we got the airplane out and didn't miss it...."

Chapter Nineteen

Low and oowvah

Every summer, the aviation buffs at Derry held an air show. Old warbirds were a local favourite. One year the show committee invited the Texas-based Confounded Air Force to fly up whatever aircraft they could spare. With the promise of "a good time", the idea caught on. The word went out to all CAF members. This was the year to visit "our Canadian friends."

The Confounded Air Force was a private, civilian organization dedicated to the restoration of World War II aircraft to flying condition. The membership consisted of mostly older men who had more money and enthusiasm than flying ability.

For the two days leading up to the air show weekend, the Derry Air staff were treated to the incredible sights and sounds of beautifully-polished piston pushers of the past arriving in groups and parking in the infield across the ramp from the flying school.

The weather was typical summer industrial — hot, muggy, and hazy. The visibility was three miles and had been for a week. The radio chatter on the Derry tower frequency invariably went something like this:

"Derrry Taawwar," the southern draw was as slow and sweet as molassas, "this is Helllcat six threee, ninnne threee, limmma. I'm leadin' a flight of threee wawrrbirds inbound, ooowvaah."

The transmission was hollow and scratchy. It sounded like it was coming from a portable radio along with the background static of 36 unshielded spark plugs. It was.

The Derry controllers were tolerant. "Six three nine three lima, roger, call on a left downwind for Runway 24; winds light and variable, altimeter 30.14."

"Six threee, ninnne threee, limmma, raawgah. Go aheaaad vectorrs to the fieeeld."

"Six three nine three lima, Derry does not have radar. I can give you the Derry NDB frequency."

"Derrry Tawwar, we don't have one of those BVDs. Do y'awl have a heading for us?"

The good ol' boys were lost. It was only by the patience and goodwill of the American radar controllers that they had made it to the Canadian border. Now they were using the standard Confounded Air Force arrival — get within radio range and call for vectors.

The Derry controller had direction finding equipment that provided headings to the field, which he gave. But the DF readout did not tell the controller the distance of the flight or whether the pilot was holding the heading, which he was not. In the meantime, the Derry Air student pilots were trying to learn how to fly with no horizon while their instructors spent most of the lesson looking for camouflage-coloured traffic flown by three grandfathers who might be coming from any direction.

Eventually the wayward trio found the field by flying close enough for the controllers to see them. "Six three nine three lima, the airport is on your left. If you turn left now, you will be on a left base for Runway 24. You are cleared to land on Runway 24."

"Six threee, ninnne threee, limmma, raawgha. We don't wanna lannnd. We wannnt a lowww and ooowvah."

The controller reluctantly cleared the flight for a low and over because he knew that they would do it anyway. It was a treat for the people on the ground. The three warbirds thundered across the field heading straight for the control tower. At the last second, the leader called on the radio, "Hellcat fliiight, breaaak leeeft — nowww!"

Two turned left and one right. It took another five minutes for the controller to gather them up again for a landing.

This went on for two days. By Friday afternoon there were 32 warbirds parked on the infield, everything from North American T-6 trainers to Boeing B-17 bombers. The crews sat in the grass in their round-bellied flight suits and braid-covered baseball caps, swapping stories with their new Canadian friends.

Someone mentioned that nearby Toronto had the tallest free-standing structure in the world, the CN Tower. It was difficult for the visitors to imagine that the largest anything would not be in Texas.

"Damn. Were is this Tarrranta place, anyway?"

"Just up the lakeshore that way."

"Come onnn, Bubbba, leeet's go see."

With that, 32 warbird pilots and their crews scrambled for their airplanes.

DERRY AIR

A quick-thinking air show organizer with a portable radio transmitter called ground control. "This is Air Show One. Ah, these guys starting their engines here want to see the CN Tower, and are going to fly to Toronto along the shoreline, over?"

Diana Bates was working the ground control position. She could see the first of the armada already starting to taxi. She handled it well. "All warbirds, this is Derry Ground, taxi to Runway 06, wind is calm, altimeter 30.06. You are cleared for takeoff when ready. Provide your own separation and stay on this frequency. You are cleared for a straight out departure. Do not reply to this transmission."

Diana repeated the call without pause. The heavy iron taxied out and took off in groups of twos and threes. In between repeating the warbird clearance, Diana redirected those of us who thought we were going to land.

"Tango Victor Hotel, the new runway for you is 28. Make a 270 degree turn to your right and call established on final. Break, break; Flight 987, your arrival will be delayed. You are cleared to orbit overhead the field at 1,500 feet. When you do, you will see 32 warplanes departing Runway 06 on a straight out."

"All right! 987 has the traffic 10 o'clock low. Looks great!"

Diana then called Toronto Centre on the direct line. "Toronto, Derry here. We have 32 antique warplanes departing 06 heading your way, low level along the shoreline. The ones with radios are staying on my frequency. I think they're going to circle the CN Tower."

The warbird fleet followed the Lake Ontario shoreline to downtown Toronto where it circled the CN Tower at the revolving restaurant level. The nearby Toronto Island Airport was forced to stop operations for about 10 minutes. No one seemed to mind. The incredible sight and awesome sound of the once-in-a-lifetime parade of antique aircraft made up for the temporary inconvenience.

On returning to Derry, the lead plane called on the radio. "Derry Tower this is waaawrbird group. We're inbound."

"All warbirds, this is Derry Tower. You are cleared to land straight in on Runway 24. Wind is calm, altimeter 30.06. Provide your own separation. Do not acknowledge this transmission."

Diana was about to repeat the message, but she was interrupted.

"Tower, we don't wanna lannd, we want a lowww and ooowvah."

Chapter Twenty

Highway robbery

Eric and Roger flew a highway patrol on a particularly steamy day in July. It was hot work. The aircraft vents were designed for faster speeds than were used during endless circling over the traffic. During the afternoon flight, Roger beat the heat by removing his police uniform piece by piece. He made a pile of clothes on the seat beside him. At the end of the two and a half hour patrol he was clad in boxer shorts only. This wouldn't make any difference to the drivers being pulled over on the ground. If they looked at the airplane overhead, they would only see his head peering down from the rear window on the left side.

That would be the end of the story except that Roger fell asleep in the back seat during the return flight to Derry. This did not escape Eric. Approaching the airport, he spoke softly to the air traffic controller and turned the radio receiver volume down. He flew a long power-on descent to the runway so there would be no change in the engine tone that might wake up the sleeping policeman. He made the smoothest landing of his life. While taxiing in, Eric gathered up the policeman's clothes from the back seat. He pulled right up to the front door of the flying school, hit the brakes, chopped the power, and jumped out with the clothes, all in one motion.

Roger woke up in the sudden silence to find a bunch of us in the Derry Air lounge staring through the windows at what appeared to be a naked policeman in the back seat of the Cessna. Eric had run past us with a bundle of clothes under his arm without saying anything.

If Eric had thought someone like Roger would be bothered by a public showing in his underwear, he was mistaken. Roger calmly climbed out of the airplane, walked through the front door, across the lounge and went looking for Eric out the other side.

He hadn't been gone long when a police cruiser came careening around to the airside ramp with all its lights flashing and siren blaring. Eric was driving and he was the only one in the car. He screeched to a halt beside the Cessna on the ramp. He climbed out and walked into the lounge carrying Roger's clothes and wearing a huge grin. Roger came back in through the rear door. He shook an accusing finger at Eric.

"I'll get you for this," he said.

As he handed Roger's uniform to him, Eric replied, "If you're hot, we could go to your house for a few beers and a swim in the pool. You're already dressed for it."

Roger grinned back as he separated each piece of uniform from the pile. "You should have kept the gun," he said.

"I took the bullets out," Eric replied, still grinning.

"Good idea."

Chapter Twenty-one

Hoser

"You realize that we're flying with these snot-nose shavetails because it's Irv's way of thanking the army for letting him out on a medical discharge."

The "snot-nosed shavetails" were four air cadets assigned to Derry Air for flying lessons in July. The speaker was Chief Instructor Eric Daedalus. He and I were teaching the cadets. I thought it was a fun job and I suspect Eric did too.

The cadets were push-button students. They were young, keen, and knew a lot about aviation already. Eric and I walked them through the course quickly, flying with each one twice a day. Their exposure was doubled by placing two cadets in the airplane for each dual lesson. One flew in the left seat while the other monitored from the back. We often had them switch seats in the air or at the side of the runway to save time. By the end of the first week the four of them were ready to fly on their own.

This brought us to the hardest part of the program — the ritual of dousing students with a bucket of water after their first solo. The first one was easy. Eric arranged for Louey the lineman to hide on the roof behind the sign over the front door. Eric sent the cadet for one circuit on his own after doing a few takeoffs and landings with him first. He walked in from the taxiway and waited for him under the sign.

The student flew the circuit, landed, taxied in and parked the aircraft. When he approached the office, Eric gave him a big handshake and hearty congratulations. Louey emptied a water bucket on his head. The other cadets thought it was great, but they saw how it was done.

The next one was mine. I hid a bucket of water under a Cherokee 140 parked on the line. When the student taxied in and shut down after his first solo flight, I pretended to be briefing one of the other cadets on parts of the airplane. We congratulated the solo student as he walked in from his aircraft. When he had passed, I pulled the bucket out and nailed him from behind.

The third one was wary, but we were ready. We recruited all three linecrew. Huey hid beside an airplane, Duey behind the gas truck and Louey around the corner of the hangar. When he was walking in from the aircraft, the student saw Huey and dodged his throw, but then the other two linecrew doused him in a beautiful crossfire.

Angel, the receptionist, had two unwritten rules about this game. The first was: "no water in the office". This meant students were home free if they made it through the front door. The second rule was: "no locking the front door". This was her idea of fair play.

The fourth air cadet was a girl. Her gender was not a factor in the ritual, but she was a little smarter and more athletic than the first three cadets.

We loaded five buckets scrounged from all corners of the hangar. They were manned by two linecrew, two air cadets and myself. Our target taxied in from her first solo and shut down on the flight line. She climbed out of the Cherokee and started walking casually to the office. When Huey came out from beside an airplane, she neatly ducked his throw and started an end-around sprint outside Duey and the gas truck. This effectively put the air cadets on our other flank out of range. That left me between her and the office door. She stopped for a moment, as if trapped. I unloaded too soon and she deeked out of the way at the last second. Savouring her victory, she stopped with one hand on the door and gave us a wave.

She never saw Mingy. When she opened the door, she was propelled backward by a wall of water. The Derry Air owner was a veteran of many cadet scholarship programs. He had unwound the fire hose from inside the hangar and walked it through the office. He stood on the other side of the glass door with the hose charged and his hand on the nozzle valve. The unsuspecting cadet opened the door and took a short blast square on. It was one of the few times I saw Mingy smile.

Chapter Twenty-two

Ready or not

Aviation is not kind to Type A personalities. It's too bad really; aggressive people could make good use of flying, but few do. Mark Warren was a Type A advertising salesman who charged into Derry Air one day looking to learn how to fly. Warren was a short, round man with slicked down, thinning hair. His open trench coat trailed behind as he slid to a stop at the flight desk. "Hello doll," he said to Angel. His voice was deep for his size. "Can a guy get flying lessons around here?"

Angel was no doll and she hated small talk. Warren had just labeled himself a "bull shooter", but Angel treated every potential customer the same. "Yes," she replied without a smile.

"That's great," he said, clapping his hands and rubbing them together. "When do I start?"

I was sitting out a cancellation and had enough time for an introductory flying lesson before my next student. Angel caught my eye. I walked over and introduced myself.

"Have you ever flown before?" I asked Warren.

"Sure, with some buddies, but I want to get a licence and buy a plane."

"Good," I said, "come over here." I motioned toward a briefing cubicle. "I'll outline some basics about the course and get you started."

"Aren't we goin' flying?" he asked.

"Yes, but we'll do a little ground briefing first." Warren reluctantly followed me.

"Mind if I smoke?" he asked as he lit a cigarette.

While I talked about learning how to fly, Warren looked around impatiently and tapped his fingers on the table. When I took him out to the aircraft, he paid more attention. In the air, he worked the controls with great enthusiasm, but he displayed little ability. He happily wandered all over the sky.

"This is easy," he declared.

"Well, there is a bit more to learning to fly than this," I said.

"Show me," he declared.

"Not right now," I said. "We have to turn back to the airport."

"So soon? Can't we cover a couple of lessons today?"

"No, I have other students, but we'll make some bookings."

Back on the ground I sold him a student kit, started his log book and signed him up for ground school. Angel said, "That'll be $545, including the flight."

Warren flipped a credit card on the counter. Angel phoned for authorization. Warren said to me, "I want to book two lessons every afternoon during the week. How soon before I go solo?"

"You need a pilot medical first," I said. "Here's Doctor Roy's phone number. He's the local designated aviation medical examiner."

"I'm fit as a fiddle," Warren claimed after taking a deep drag of his cigarette.

"They won't take it," Angel said, flipping Warren's credit card back on the counter.

"You'll need the medical anyway," I said.

Warren tossed Angel another card. "Try this," he said "and see if you can get me a medical with this doctor, today, will ya babe?"

"I can book you three afternoon lessons this week," I said, looking at our appointment sheets. "Before our next lesson tomorrow, read the first nine chapters in the Flying Training Manual in your kit."

"They won't take it," Angel said, returning the second credit card.

Warren pulled another one from his wallet and handed it to her. I could see he had more.

The third card was accepted. Angel telephoned Dr. Roy's office. They said they could take him at the end of the week.

"Thanks, sweetheart."

In the ground briefing the next day, it was obvious that Warren hadn't read the Flying Training Manual. I stretched the briefing out to cover the material, but he didn't pay much attention. In the air he sawed away at the controls with little positive results.

"How am I doin'?" he asked.

"Not bad," I lied.

"Thought so," he said, "I've never had trouble mastering anything in my life."

By the end of the week, Warren had not made much progress in the air, but was still keen. His credit card companies were not. His bill for Friday's lesson was $105. It took six cards before one would authorize the amount.

On Monday, the weather was bad, but Warren came out anyway.

"How did your medical go?" I asked.

"The Doc said I was fine," Warren replied.

"Good. You'll receive a form from the government in two weeks. Bring it in. We need it for your Student Pilot Permit."

"Two weeks! You mean I can't go solo for two more weeks? Can't you speed that up?"

"Not really. We have some other things to cover in the meantime," I said.

"Like what?"

"Like the government and our company pre-solo examinations. These are multiple choice exams on air regulations and other facts you should know before your first solo."

"I'll write them now," he said taking out his cigarettes and pulling off his trench coat. "Let's go."

I gave him the Derry Air Pre-solo Exam. He answered eight questions out of 25 correctly. I reviewed his mistakes, which was all that was required. The government exam wasn't as easy. He got five right out of 50. A pass was 45. I corrected his mistakes. He had to write it until he obtained a pass.

"I'll write it again now," he declared.

"I don't think so," I said. "When you do it again, it won't be the same exam." He agreed to wait.

We did three flying lessons that week. The material I covered in the air was really just the first three lessons rearranged for review. Warren was happy to fly, but he wasn't making much progress. By Friday, none of Warren's credit card companies would cover his bill. It was no problem for Angel. She split the invoice into three parts and received authorization for the smaller amounts.

"I'll be near the government office on Monday," Warren said. "I'll pick up my Student Pilot Permit if it's ready."

"I'll call them," I said.

The government had no record of Mark Warren. They had not received his medical application. I phoned Dr. Roy's office. His receptionist answered.

"Have you sent out Mark Warren's medical yet?" I asked.

"No. He paid by cheque. It bounced. Now he'll have to pay the returned cheque charge and the medical in cash."

I told Warren what she had said. "You take care of that and I'll see you on Monday. You can rewrite the government exam after your lesson."

"Okay." He didn't sound his usual hard-charging self.

Warren didn't show up for his lesson Monday and didn't return my calls. I mentioned to Angel that it was too bad as he was really keen to fly. Before she could comment, a familiar voice came over the office control tower monitor. It was Warren in an aircraft belonging to Condor Aviation.

"Derry Tower, I'm ready for take off. Let's get this show on the road."

His debt kept him from flying at Derry Air so he just switched schools. He was now burning both ends of the candle at Condor.

Chapter Twenty-three

The flying horseman

Susan and I went horse back riding on one of the rare days off that we had together. She was right about Sunny. He was a sweetheart. He stood quietly while I saddled him and cinched the girth. He opened his mouth to take the bit and he stood patiently beside the corral fence while I used it to climb on.

We headed up a dirt road to the bush at the back of the property across from us. It was obvious that Sunny's legs were bothering him. His walk was stilted. No amount of urging would make him catch up to Cricket who was surging eagerly ahead.

Susan reined in her young horse. "He'll go better once he loosens up," she said. "Let him have his own pace."

Off the sideroad, there was an abandoned logging path cut through the bush. We turned the horses onto it. Sunny gradually picked up the speed of his walk.

"Does he feel like he's ready for a trot?" Susan called out from ahead.

Sunny heard and understood. Years of lessons had taught him the language of riding. He broke into a trot before I could answer. His motion was smooth. His workhorse hooves clopped noisily in the dirt. Cricket flattened her ears back and increased her speed.

The twin tracks through the bush were wide but old and unused. Saplings growing in the middle slapped at the horses' legs. Occasionally overhanging branches swiped at our heads. We didn't know how far the road went but it was fairly straight. Susan let Cricket break into a canter on her own. Sunny matched the pace. It was exciting being on top of a half ton animal that moved so easily. I could feel his power through my legs which were clamped tightly around him. The flat English saddle offered no security for a novice rider.

Sunny's big hooves were pounding the path now. Cricket went faster. Sunny pulled up beside her easily with his great loping strides.

I was beginning to feel like I was living the life of a squire. I pretended that I was charging through bush, racing my wife on our own huge estate. Life couldn't be better.

Life quickly got worse. The horses were near a gallop and Sunny was pulling ahead when we rounded a turn. A hundred feet ahead there was a large tree laying across the path. The property owner might have put it there to discourage snowmobilers and horseback riders from using his bush.

The reactions of Cricket and Sunny were simultaneous and opposite. The young horse immediately put on the brakes. The old show jumper lifted his head to see over the fat tree trunk, put his ears forward and accelerated. Susan realized what was coming long before I did.

"Rein him in," she yelled.

It was too late. In three great strides, Sunny closed the gap to the tree and launched both of us into the air. I had never flown a horse. On the rise, I flopped onto his neck. A regular horse would have been driven down with my weight on his head but Sunny had the power and momentum to carry us both over the tree. He easily cleared a five-foot barrier of trunk and branches. On the down side of the jump, I was thrown back onto Sunny's rump with my feet still in the stirrups. When he landed, I bounced twice on his back and then fell off. It seemed like a long time before I hit the dirt.

Initially nothing hurt. A rush of adrenaline made me giddy. A replay of what the whole scenario must have looked like flashed through my mind.

Susan scrambled over the tree to find me stretched out on my back well down the path, laughing hilariously while Sunny stood over me looking bewildered.

"Are you all right?" she called.

I couldn't answer her right away. I was laughing too hard.

I wasn't really hurt. Bruised, yes; broken, no. Once we both figured this out, Susan started to laugh.

"I wish I could've seen your face," she said between gaffaws. "But from behind, it was funny enough. You and Sunny could do a comedy riding act but I don't think you'd live very long."

Our next problem was retracing our route. Susan and I could climb back over the tree but Sunny couldn't. The bush was swampy on either side. We stood there looking around.

"I'll jump him going the other way," Susan finally said.

"Are you sure?" I asked.

"No. I've never jumped that high, but Sunny obviously has. If he's good for it, so am I."

It didn't sound like a good idea but I didn't have a better one. Susan had made up her mind, so I didn't argue. I climbed the log. Cricket was tied to a branch on the other side. I took the reins and led her up the path. I figured that she would spook when Sunny and Susan came flying over.

I heard them coming long before I saw Susan's head bobbing toward the barrier from the other side. Sunny launched for her just as he had for me, but she knew what to do. She stayed crouched forward as they sailed over the tree. I could see her wide eyes and huge grin from well back.

Susan let out a "whoop" when they landed. She reined Sunny to a stop beside us. She was pretty excited.

"Want to ride Cricket?" she asked.

"Sure," I said. "She's a lot closer to the ground."

Chapter Twenty-four

Boner

I flew the Highway Patrol on a holiday Monday so Eric Daedalus could take the day off. He told me what to do.

"Just fly the designated section along the right side of the highway at 80 knots about 1,000 feet above ground. The cop will sit behind you and watch the traffic coming the other way. When he spots a violation, he'll call it out. You turn around and follow the car. Down the road a cop on the ground will wave it over. You circle while the guy in the airplane reads out the violation through the other cop's portable radio. The hardest part of the job is staying awake."

The "cop" was Roger Shirley, the Highway Patrol regular. We had a coffee together before departing on the first of two flights.

"Holidays are usually boring," Shirley said. "The high volume of traffic slows everything down but today we have Constable Boner on the ground. He's too new and too keen. This could be interesting."

We took off and flew to the designated area outside of town. I set the Cessna in a maximum endurance cruise in a lazy racetrack pattern around four, one-mile marks on the pavement of the four-lane highway. Constable Boner was standing next to a police cruiser parked down the road.

Shirley was right. It was impossible for anyone to speed through the solid lines of holiday traffic. Most of our time was wasted circling a law-abiding stream of vehicles. We flew nearly an hour before a jeep pulled onto the shoulder of the road and used it for a passing lane.

"Turn and follow the grey jeep on the gravel," Shirley said. "Then keep your eye on Boner up the road."

The jeep driver saw the police car well ahead and pulled back into the traffic, but Shirley already had him pegged.

"Grey jeep, Boner," Shirley said into the radio. "He's two miles back in the driving lane. The charge will be improper passing on a highway."

I could see Boner walking toward the edge of the asphalt.

"He's one mile from you now, Boner, behind the white delivery van. If you can't get him, don't worry about it."

Boner was standing close to the road. The highway traffic parading past him in the driving lane had to be close to his toes.

"He's coming to you now, Boner."

As the jeep approached, the cop on the ground actually leaned into the traffic, pointed his finger at the driver and motioned for him to pull onto the shoulder of the road. We could see it all plainly from 1,000 feet above.

It took the driver a distance to get stopped on the gravel. Boner faithfully trotted after him.

"Vigilante," Shirley muttered.

"Why do you call him that?" I asked.

"He takes this job too seriously. It's as if each offender is a criminal that must be caught. These are traffic violations, not homicides. I'll be surprised if he doesn't get run over before the day is out."

When Boner reached the stopped jeep, Shirley read the citation to the driver via the portable radio in the other cop's shirt pocket. Boner wrote out the ticket and gave it to him.

We stopped two other vehicles during the rest of the two and a half hour patrol. Both cars were riding the bumpers of the ones ahead and were cited for following too close. Each time Boner reached into the traffic to wave them over.

Shirley called a lunch break. We flew back to Derry Air and Boner met us at Nicks Restaurant in the airport terminal building. Shirley introduced us. Boner was tall, young and muscular. A blond crew cut topped a small head with cauliflower ears on massive shoulders. He smiled like an unsuspecting puppy. When we sat down to eat, he straddled the chair and placed his gun on one side of his plate and his night stick on the other.

Shirley looked at me and said, "In fifteen years on the force I have never drawn my gun on duty. Boner pulls it out to guard his French fries."

The young cop grinned.

"Put the gun away, Boner. There are no potato robbers in this restaurant. I checked."

Boner frowned and slid his sidearm back into its holster.

"Thank you," Shirley said.

Not much was said during the rest of the lunch. Before we left, Shirley suggested to Boner that he be less zealous when fingering traffic violators.

"I don't mind if you get run over, Boner, but I worry that someone will swerve to miss you and hit another car."

On the way back to the patrol area, Shirley commented on Boner's intelligence. "I think the police academy gives new candidates an IQ test. If they fail, they're hired."

It was obvious during the afternoon patrol that Shirley was reluctant to call out a violation. He was nodding off to sleep behind me when I spotted a red Porsche trying to go faster than everyone else by weaving in and out of traffic.

"See the Porsche?" I asked. The question woke Shirley.

"Got it," he replied.

The sports car looked like it was trying to push a Buick up the road.

"Red Porsche, Boner," Shirley called into the radio. "It's three miles back, right lane. The charge will be following too close and failing to signal a lane change."

"Roger," crackled the reply.

"Two miles, Boner. It's now in the left lane.

"Coming up to one mile, Boner ... okay, forget it, Boner. It's passing a school bus. I don't want you to stop it." Shirley was speaking loudly and clearly. "LET IT GO, BONER."

Constable Boner ignored the order. He was set on getting his man. He stepped in front of the school bus, which was now 100 metres away from him travelling at 80 kilometres an hour. He stuck his hand up, signaling the bus to stop. Then he pointed at the Porsche with his other hand and waved it over to his side of the road.

The bus driver had three choices, none of which was to stop in the distance remaining. He could either hit the cop, hit the Porsche, or go off the road. He went off the road, locking up the wheels and turning the bus sideways in the process. Several drivers behind him had to do the same thing. The Porsche driver was smart enough to keep going. When the dust settled, there were six vehicles off the road. Miraculously none were damaged.

Shirley chewed out Boner over the radio and then said to me, "It'll take him a while to sort that one out; let's call it a day."

Chapter Twenty-five

Coffee to go

The linecrew at Derry Air changed shifts at 14:30 every day. Huey, Duey and Louey alternated mornings and afternoons with the Three Stooges, a nickname affectionately and accurately applied by the rest of the flying school staff to Dean, Mumbles and Crazy Jim.

The linecrew divided their time between Derry Air, the terminal ramp and Nicks, the terminal building coffee shop. Their job was to service the flying school and charter airplanes as well as the six to eight airline flights a day that stopped at Derry.

The Derry Airport Terminal was a modern but small single storey glass and steel building. It contained an airline counter for two carriers, two gates, a rental car kiosk, a customs office and the coffee shop.

The building was at the other end of the hangar line from Derry Air, out of sight of manager, Mingy. Nicks was a favorite place for the linecrew to hide whether they were working or not.

One day the second shift started by unloading baggage from an airline flight. The first shift retired to Nicks.

Crazy Jim was driving the ancient Ford tractor that was used to pull the baggage carts. He was headed back to the terminal with four loaded wagons when he spotted Huey, Duey and Louey sitting in the coffee shop by the airside window. Just for fun he aimed the tractor and the loaded train straight at them. He was going flat out in second gear. At the last second, Jim slammed on the old Ford's brakes.

The tractor said, "No!" The master brake cylinder blew out and the whole train plunged unabated into the restaurant.

It was a testament to the flimsy engineering of the terminal building that no one was seriously hurt. The tractor easily punched through the thin steel and glass wall. It hit the linecrew table square on, pushing it and its three occupants across the small room stopping the length of a full baggage cart into the room with Jim still on board. Steam from the tractor radiator rose from the wreckage. Nick called the airport fire crew. They foamed the whole mess.

I didn't see it happen, but Nick told the story to every customer who came into the restaurant for months afterward. Whenever anyone looked at the blue boat cover that was hanging over the hole to keep the weather out until repairs could be made, Nick would launch into a story that got longer and more exciting with each telling.

Mingy hauled the rest of them into his office for a lecture. Dutch got wind of what was going on and barged in. Mingy was hot under the collar because he believed the linecrew were careless. Dutch argued that the equipment he gave them was second rate. Mingy threatened to fire them all. Dutch ended the argument and won it at the same time by saying there would be no one to service the next airline flight which was due in ten minutes. I heard Dutch's parting shot as he came out of the office.

"And they'll need to borrow your new pick-up truck to tow da baggage carts. Da tractor is broken."

Chapter Twenty-six

Tit for tat

"You're going to send me solo today, aren't you?" Diana Bates asked. We were walking out to the airplane on the day I was planning to send her on a first solo flight.

"Oh, I don't know," I lied. She was a good student. There was no reason not to send her on her own.

Instructors normally spring this flight on their students at the last minute. Then the students don't have a chance to get nervous about it but Diana had seen the routine played out from the control tower many times.

"First you'll do a few circuits with me to satisfy the insurance company," she said. "Are you going to stop beside the runway and give me a pep talk before I go?"

"What is this?" I protested, "a demonstration of women's intuition?"

"Maybe."

"If I told you that you were going solo today, you'd get nervous and fly lousy. Then I wouldn't be able to send you and you'd develop an inferiority complex." I said the last part just to get even with her for second guessing my lesson plan. Diana was six feet tall and smart. Inferior was not in her vocabulary.

"Not a chance," she said.

She flew three perfect circuits. I called for a full stop landing.

"Do you want a ride back to the ramp or are you getting out here?" she asked when we pulled off the runway.

"I'll walk. I need the exercise," I replied. "You know what to do?"

"Affirmative and thank you for teaching me well," she said. "Now get out."

I walked to the office to sign the first solo certificate and listen to the radio. The only other traffic was a Piper Twin Comanche. It was Bull Muldoone on his third Instrument Rating Flight Test. He had easily failed the first two before the rides were over, but was nearing the end of this one. To finish the test,

95

Bull had to fly the localizer backcourse approach to Runway 24 at the Derry Airport. The inspector simulated a right engine failure and a landing gear malfunction. Bull handled it well enough to hold the localizer to the visual approach point. He only had to complete a circling approach to Runway 06 without rolling the airplane inverted and he would pass the ride.

The unlikeable loudmouth had correctly eased to the right for the left hand circling approach. This put him behind Diana's Cherokee flying on the left downwind leg of her first solo. Diana called for a full stop. The controller cleared her to land. Bull called downwind. I could hear the landing gear horn blaring and the good engine roaring at full power in the background of his radio transmission. I could imagine him using full left rudder to keep straight against the left engine and milking the nose attitude to hold the minimum single-engine speed. There was a touch of desperation in Bull's voice. His speed was 20 knots faster than Diana's and he was gobbling up the space between the airplanes.

The tower controller said, "You're number two."

Bull was flying on the edge and in danger of losing it all. The Twin Comanche didn't have enough reserve performance on one engine to allow him to turn toward the dead engine again to widen his circuit.

"Derry Tower, I'm doing a simulated single-engine approach here." He was trying to sound calm but it wasn't working. "Perhaps the little lady in the Cherokee would like to overshoot and get out of my way."

The controller did not respond. He left it all up to Diana. I knew her quite well by then. Bull shouldn't have called her a "little lady."

"Tell the other pilot," Diana replied calmly, "that I'm also on a single-engine approach."

Chapter Twenty-seven

Alumnus

Ray Tragunno was a Derry Air alumnus. He had started his aviation career as an instructor at the flying school. Ray then worked his way into the charter department and accumulated enough multi-engine flying hours to top the hiring list on a major airline. The air carrier trained him as a second officer on Boeing 747s.

Ray worked three days a week. He flew to Europe one day, stayed over for another and flew back on the third. Then, according to his union contract, he was time expired until the next week. If the weather was bad on his days off, Ray visited Derry Air. He knew there would be instructors to talk flying to over a coffee. Henry and I were an eager audience during these "hangar" sessions. We wanted the airlines to hire us so we could wear a nice uniform, fly Jumbo jets, talk with a deep voice and have time off to hang around the local flying school. When Ray came to Derry Air we bought his coffee and pumped him for information. Ray's responses were always entertaining.

Henry was closer to qualifying for an airline job than me. One day he asked Ray about the hiring interviews.

"The first interview was pretty standard," Ray said. "It included a physical examination, inside and out, if you know what I mean, and an interview with the personnel manager. Then there were aptitude and IQ tests. I think you have to fail them to qualify. A shifty-eyed shrink gave the second interview. He asked tricky questions like, 'Do you love your mother?' I assumed if you answered 'Yes', he would note that you're an insecure mama's boy. If you said 'No', then you'd be labeled an insecure woman hater. I told him that my mother had passed away but on her death bed she had made me promise to be an airline pilot."

"I didn't know your mother had died," Henry said. "I'm sorry to hear that."

"She would be too," Ray replied, "so don't tell her I said it."

DERRY AIR

"The final interview was the most interesting. There was a panel of five: the personnel manager, the shrink and three senior airline captains."

Henry and I got nervous just thinking about standing before such a panel and staking our careers on their first impressions.

"The personnel manager introduced everyone, read my background and explained that each pilot would ask a question. The first one painted a verbal picture. He asked me what I would do if I was flying a 747 in the mountains, had lost the left two engines, had a fire indication in the aft galley and knew the weather at the nearest airport was below IFR limits.

"I told him that I didn't have a clue. I said that I had never been in a 747 but I hoped when the airline hired me that I would be paired with a qualified captain such as himself who knew what to do.

"The second guy asked me to describe my most memorable day in aviation. I told him it was when I got laid in a Piper Super Cub flying at 5,280 feet over Niagara Falls.

"The last pilot asked what I would say if I was being interviewed to fly Cherokee 140s on a new airline service that only runs the 50 miles between Derry and Toronto and back."

Henry and I could see ourselves convincing the panel that we'd be pleased to fly their Cherokees. We'd tell them anything as long as it got our feet in the door to fly their airliners.

Not Ray.

"I told them that I had already done the small airplane thing. If I was being interviewed to fly single-engine aircraft from Derry to Toronto that they could shove their Cherokees where the sun doesn't shine."

"Wow! What did he say?" Henry asked.

"He didn't say anything. He just smiled. The personnel manager thanked me and I left. He called me a week later and said I got the job."

Chapter Twenty-eight

Know-it-all

Some people were born to be difficult. At Derry Air junior instructors were hired to fly with them.

"I want you to do Keith Harrison's dual cross-country," Eric Daedalus told me one morning. He was grinning.

Keith Harrison was a student pilot and a middle-aged know-it-all. I had heard the other instructors refer to him as a handful but I didn't have a full slate of bookings. I couldn't refuse.

"Thanks a bunch," I replied.

"You're welcome," he said. "My best advice is that the man can fly better than either of us, so just relax and enjoy the ride."

The Derry Air student dual cross-country was a two-hour triangular course. It went southwest to the town of Pie on the north shore of Lake Erie, then north to Kitchener and back. It could be a simple flight except the government required student pilots to learn every navigation trick invented since Charles Lindbergh had flown open cockpits. The lesson had become a complicated half-day affair.

Before doing their dual cross-country, students had already taken navigation ground school and had been given an initial planning briefing. They arrived for the flight laden with a map, a book of airport information, pilot operating handbook, ruler, protractor, circular and/or electronic computer, stopwatch, knee-board, weather reports, a two-page flight plan and assorted notched pencils. Their maps were covered with multi-coloured course and drift angles and cross marks for distance. Some students tied everything around their necks; a few bought flight suits and used all the zippered pockets.

Harrison arrived wearing sneakers, jeans and a faded Gordon Lightfoot T-shirt. He was carrying a flight plan form and a naked map. There was a pencil stuck behind his ear.

"All set?" he asked with a smirk.

"I am, but what about you?"

"Ready to go, chief," he replied.

"Did you check the weather?" I asked.

He ducked down to look at the clear blue sky through the lounge window. "Yup."

"Have you filed a flight plan?"

"Flight Itinerary with the wife," he replied.

"That works until she wants to collect your life insurance," I said.

"Pardon me?"

"Never mind."

I decided if this man wanted to launch on his first cross-country unprepared, I'd let him. He could fall on his face and then I'd make him do the lesson over again.

"On the first leg," I said, "I'd like you to map read, check drift and calculate our ground speed. By half-way, give me the final heading that will take us to the first destination and our estimated time of arrival."

"Whatever you say, chief."

I signed us out and went with him to check over the aircraft. Harrison's pre-flight of the Cherokee was as minimal as his flight planning. We both climbed in. I sat there quietly while he fired up the engine, called the ground controller for taxi instructions and headed for the runway.

Student pilots are taught to depart on a cross-country from a set heading point along the way and then cruise 10 miles or so for drift and ground speed checks. Harrison's takeoff into the wind happened to be in the opposite direction to our course. He turned and climbed out parallel to the runway.

"The final heading to Pie is 255 degrees," he said, "and our ETA is 10:40." He was wearing that stupid grin again.

"That's it?" I asked. "No further calculations required?"

"Nope."

"Okay," I replied, "we'll see when we get there."

Harrison told me later that he got the estimates by flying the downwind leg along the 6,000-foot runway. This allowed him to check his ground speed against our climb speed and then apply a correction to the predetermined cruise speed. For drift, he flew parallel to the runway and then checked where we crossed Derry's intersecting runway. He fudged how this would change in the stronger winds aloft.

I had flown the route with other students so I soon knew that Harrison was bang on with his calculations. So did he. He sat back and looked pleased with himself. I pulled the throttle to idle.

"Simulated engine failure," I announced.

Harrison pushed the throttle back in. "There, all fixed," he said.

I pulled the power off again and said, "Let's do the whole drill," I said, "You can have the power back when we reach 500 feet."

Harrison set up a glide and flew a perfect deadstick approach to a field while completing the emergency checks. I restored the power. During the climbout I said, "When you are back on course, give me a revised ETA to Pie."

He climbed out to the point where we had started the forced approach and added the time we had taken on the drill to his original ETA. "10:51," he said. He was right.

Normally we stopped at Pie to brief the students before the next leg. I told Harrison to do a touch and go.

"Fly the next leg at 500 feet," I said, hoping to throw him off. "I'll need an ETA."

"11:34," he replied immediately. He told me later that he simply used his flight planned time since it had proved accurate on the first leg.

His low level map reading was flawless. We arrived at Kitchener on time and on course.

"Do another touch and go," I said.

I decided to change my tactics. "Well, there is nothing I can teach you about navigation, Keith," I said. "Take us home. You're a good pilot."

"I know," he replied.

While Harrison was climbing out toward Derry, I took my headset off and placed it on top of the instrument panel near the compass. The magnetic microphone in the headset forced a 50-degree swing to the right.

"Check your heading indicator," I said. Then I pretended to go to sleep.

Harrison reset the heading indicator to the faulty compass reading and turned to follow it. The new course carried us back toward Pie but was far enough off to take us over new territory. It was all farm country. There were no significant landmarks along the route.

The City of Derry is on the shore of Lake Ontario. About the time we should have been there, we came to Lake Erie. I pretended to wake up. For once Harrison looked seriously unsure of himself but he brightened up when he saw a town in the distance further to the right. "Derry," he said, hopefully.

"Let's go see," I replied.

As we got closer, he could see the town was familiar but it wasn't Derry. I picked up my headset and spoke into the intercom.

"Pie," I said.

"No way," he said, but then he saw the Pie Airport. He knew I was right.

"I don't understand it," he said. "I know everything about navigation."

"You know a lot about navigation," I corrected, "but you don't know everything. If you can take us home from here without further difficulty, I'll sign you off for your solo cross-country so you can practise more."

"Thank you," he said nervously. He was still puzzled over what had happened.

"You're welcome," I replied. I never told him.

Chapter Twenty-nine

Da cow flew over da moon

I was making slow progress with my farm boy student Melville Passmore. He was okay with the flying but whenever I started on the theory of things, his eyes would glaze over and he'd look worried. He didn't seem to have the brain power to grasp my explanations. I didn't know how I was going to get him past the complexity of cross-country navigation. I asked Dutch Van-DerHoven for suggestions.

"Do you know Melville is in da ground school classes?" he asked.

"Sure. That must be hard going for him and you," I replied.

At the time Dutch was running ground school sessions two nights a week. I knew that Melville was in both classes and that this was not his first time around.

"Melville is teaching da class," Dutch declared.

"He's what?" I exclaimed.

"He teach a little bit of da practical stuff in each class," Dutch said.

"I don't believe you."

"Dat's what I tought. You pretty-boy instructors t'ink you know it all. You don't. Flying should be easy. You instructors and your textbooks make it hart."

He took a breath but I didn't say anything. I knew Dutch was on a roll.

"How much hay and grain to feed a beef cow for da vinter?"

"You're asking me?"

"Yah."

"I don't know."

"Melville knows. What's da gap on distributor points in a Ford tractor?"

"How would I know?"

"Ask Melville, he knows, and furdder more, he didn't learn dat in a book. He built a shed vithout da plans and predict da veather from da sky. He knows enough to come in out of da rain and dat's more dan you can say for dose pretty-boy teenagers born vit a silver bell in deir mouts."

"Silver spoon," I corrected.

"Silver spoon, silver bell, it doesn't madder. I tell dem vere to stick it and it's not in der mouts!"

He took another breath so I jumped in.

"I agree that Melville is not stupid but you have to admit that he is slow."

It was a mistake.

"You're da vun who's slow. You try to fill his head vit da teory. Dis flying is not rocket science. Melville's a farmer. Use your noggin," Dutch said, rapping me on the head.

I hesitated to say anything else, but I couldn't tell where this conversation was going.

"So what should I do?"

"I take Melville out to da hangar and point to da parts of da aircraft. He never miss one. I take him outside and he tell me all about da clouds. I don't try to put in da head vat not dere."

"But what about navigation? How is he going to learn the circular computer?"

"Computer, smuter," Dutch exclaimed. "A smart boy like dat don't need a fancy wiz wheel to figure how not to run out of da gas! I ask him, 'If a cow valked at five miles per hour, how long vould it take to valk ten miles?' He says, 'Two hours.'

"'If you feed da cow two flakes of hay for every hour of valking, how many flakes to valk five miles?' He says, 'Two flakes.'

"Den I do da airplane. I say, 'If da airplane is flying at 100 miles in an hour, how long to go 200 miles?' He says 'Two hours?'

"'How long to go fifty miles?' 'Half an hour?'

"See? He knows. He yust doesn't know dat he knows. You have to show him."

"Okay, I'll try it."

I could see the logic in what Dutch was telling me. It would take a long time to teach someone to fly that way, but it had to be better than the near zero progress I was making now.

I formed a mental picture of Melville teaching 20 adults the parts of the airplane. The more I thought about it, the more it fit. I could imagine him pointing to each piece with his grubby fingers, keenly describing their function and then hanging his long tongue out between sentences. Something else occurred to me. Melville was sitting through the ground school lessons over and over again while waiting for his turn to teach. The old Dutchman was pretty smart.

I arranged a practice ground briefing lesson with Melville in preparation for our dual cross-country flight. At Dutch's suggestion, I told him to leave his computer, protractor and calculator in his student kit. I gave him a sample cross-country to flight plan using only a map, a pencil and a ruler. He did it. He quickly estimated accurate tracks and distances for the route and wrote them on one of the standard Derry Air flight planning forms. Then I asked him to check with the weather office for the forecast winds aloft. Applying the winds to the flight plan was the hardest part of the lesson.

Melville stayed in his seat.

"If we're goin' to fly at 4,500 feet," he said quietly, "the winds would be from the west at 20 knots."

"You checked already?" I asked.

Melville blushed.

"What? Where did you get the winds?"

"I just know," he said shyly.

"You don't just know. The information has to come from somewhere."

"The sky tells me," Melville said. He spoke softly, like it was a secret.

"Just for fun, Melville, I'm going to call the weather office and get the winds aloft. You pretend that your winds are correct and start figuring how they would affect this sample flight. I'll be back in a minute."

I called the weather office. The winds at 3,000 feet were forecast to be 260 at 15 knots. At 6,000 feet, they were to be 290 at 23. Melville was right on. I went back to our briefing cubicle.

"You were right Melville. Tell me, how does the sky tell you the winds aloft?"

He looked down at the floor. I could see he was embarrassed.

"I think it's really neat that you're tuned to nature like that. How do you do it?"

"I watch the clouds every day. Some go this way; some go that. I get to know the winds."

"Okay. Now let's apply them to our sample cross-country flight."

"I already did," he said quietly. He pushed the planning form across the table. The boxes for times enroute, heading and fuel consumption had been filled with Melville's unmistakable jagged script using his stubby pencil. He had done it during the few minutes I had been talking to the weather office. I checked the numbers in my head. They seemed okay.

"How did you do this?" I asked. I was amazed.

"Dutch taught me how to estimate everything. We practised a lot."

"This is great, Melville," I said. He beamed at the compliment. "Let's book a cross-country flight."

"Yes sir!"

I thanked Dutch for steering me right with Melville. "I would have never guessed that you could teach a farmer to fly by relating it to cow feed. Thanks for the tips."

"You never heard of da cow dat fly over da moon?"

"The cow jumped over the moon," I corrected.

"Melville and I grew up on da farm. Ve know dat cows can't jump but you can teach anyone to fly."

Chapter Thirty

Free fall

It was the makings for a good prank. Three of us were working late. Eric, Henry and I were flying with students working on their Night Ratings. We all finished at 10:30. It was a clear, cold night; there was a full moon.

Eric helped Henry and me push the airplanes into the hangar.

"How about a jump tonight, Eric?" Henry asked our roly-poly boss.

I had heard about this before. Henry talked Eric into skydiving from one of the school airplanes at night after the Derry control tower had closed. It was strictly illegal, which was why they did it. As an ex-military paratrooper, Eric loved to fly, but he lived to jump.

Eric grinned. "The last time we did that, I landed in the vineyard."

"This time, keep your legs crossed," Henry offered.

"No, tonight I think I'd rather just go to Roger's for a beer."

Roger, Eric's laugh-a-minute cop friend, lived near the airport.

"You know the UFO reports in the paper?" Henry asked.

"Yah."

"Well, I bought some flares. I thought you could do a spinning free fall with one in each hand. Derry would have its own UFO."

Eric laughed at the thought. I could tell he liked the idea. Henry kept the pressure on.

"The control tower will be closing in twenty minutes. I'll take the door off the Cessna 172."

"Oh, I don't know." Eric was hesitating.

"I'll pay for half the flight," Henry said.

"I'll pay the other half," I added.

"Why are you guys so anxious to see me try and kill myself?" Eric asked.

Henry responded by pulling two highway flares out of his

107

back pocket and handing them to Eric. "It'll be fun."

The big CFI conceded. He went to the office for his skydiving gear while I helped Henry remove the Cessna's right hand door.

Eric waddled out wearing a bulky jump suit, his parachute, a helmet and goggles. He looked like a mutant beetle. I helped him into the open side of the 172 and then headed to the office. Inside I could hear Henry's calls to Derry ground control on the office monitor.

They taxied out, did a run-up and called the tower for takeoff. The controller cleared them and said he was closing down for the night.

Ten minutes later Henry announced on the radio that they were at 8,000 feet. I went outside. Henry must have shut off the airplane's navigation lights. I couldn't see him but I could hear the engine straining at full power straight overhead. The noise soon died. At the same time, the light of the flares appeared above.

When Eric jumped, the effect was perfect. He held a flare in each glove and spun. It was like seeing a fireworks pinwheel plummeting through the sky from two kilometres up. As the free fall continued, a light breeze drifted Eric toward the other side of the airport. The spinning lights descended well past the point where I thought Eric should have popped his chute. There was a chance that he had separated himself from the flares, but the plan had been to hang on so they would descend slowly with him.

I watched as the flares continued to drop unabated into the ground on the other side of the airport. A sinking, sickening feeling spread over me as I realized that I might have witnessed Eric skydiving to his death. I ran into the flying school office and called Henry on the radio.

"We might have a problem here Henry. On your way down, see if you can spot where the flares landed."

"I can see them over by the sewage lagoon," Henry replied. "What's the problem?"

"I'll tell you on the ground," I said. "Make it quick."

I met the airplane on the ramp. When Henry shut it down, I told him what might have happened.

"Holy ....!"

We drove to the sewage lagoon and left the car with its lights flashing as a signal. The soggy field was knee deep in weeds. We shuffled along with the effluent smell wafting over us. It was spooky to think that the next form illuminated by our pocket flashlights might be the mangled body of our friend.

In the meantime, our "friend" was drinking beers with Officer Roger Shirley at his house. Roger's large back yard was well illuminated by flood lights around the outdoor swimming pool. During Eric's free fall, he had sent the flares spinning off on their own, deployed his chute and paraglided over to Roger's yard. This was not a difficult feat for a man who had been trained by the army for night insertions behind enemy lines.

He knew we would be wondering what had happened to him. When Henry and I were about to give up our search and call the police, a cruiser arrived at the lagoon. The right side window was rolled down and a familiar round face, split with a wide grin, spoke, "Are you guys ready for a beer?"

Chapter Thirty-one

I'm here to help you

This time Derry's chief meteorologist Peter Tyler sounded sincere. He said the low ceiling and fog would lift. He had reports of clearing to the west to back him up. The Derry Air lounge was filled with pilots who were counting on the weatherman's optimism so they could go flying. In the training cubicles, Henry and Eric were giving their students extended ground briefings. Bull Muldoone, the air service's resident loudmouth customer, was holding court with two buddies in a corner. His Piper Twin Comanche squatted outside on the ramp under an overload of camping gear and beer. They were waiting to fly north on a fishing trip.

I had given my student a pre-solo exam to write and was standing at the coffee maker with Brad Milton. Brad was a middle-aged, soft-spoken salesman for an American chemical company. He was a regular Derry Air customer. He had flown up from Pennsylvania in his Cessna Skylane ahead of the bad weather on one of his monthly visits to Derry's steel mills. He was waiting to fly back.

Everyone at the air service liked Brad. He treated less-than-beautiful Angel as if she was special. He talked to our linecrew, Huey, Duey and Louey as if they were intelligent. He got surprising results. Right now he was pretending to be interested in my latest hair-raising flying instructor story.

While we were talking, a white mini-van pulled up by the door to the airside ramp. A small government logo was painted on the side of the truck along with the title, "Aviation Regulatory Enforcement, Ramp Check." I'd seen the van before. It was used by government inspectors to make surprise visits to airports. They checked aircraft documents and pilot licences and looked for overloads and maintenance problems.

The inspector's arrival did not pose a problem for Derry Air. Angel maintained the company's aircraft log books and documents. They were always up-to-date and in perfect order.

Her encyclopedic mind knew the total times, expiry dates, and time-to-maintenance of all ten aircraft and their components. She coordinated the maintenance with Darcy, our chief engineer. I had never heard of her being caught out.

Bull Muldoone recognized that the van was a problem for him. Angel did not maintain his aircraft log book and neither did he. He hoisted his bulk from a grateful chair and waved his buddies through the side door. "Come on, let's find some beers."

The inspector climbed out of the van. I had met him before. He was standard government issue: medium-build, straight spine and thinning hair. He looked like an undertaker. He entered the front door and approached Angel.

"I'm Inspector Kennedy from Aviation Enforcement," he said. He was smiling as if he had gas.

The receptionist knew why he was there. She flexed the wart on her nose and pushed a stack of log books toward him. She didn't reply.

"I understand that you run a tight ship here," he said pleasantly enough. Angel nodded at the books and went back to her work.

While Kennedy picked up the first book, Brad Milton excused himself from our conversation and went out to his aircraft. He returned with his aircraft log book and documents and spread them out on the coffee table. It didn't take inspector Kennedy long to get tired of looking at Angel's perfect handwriting. He walked toward Brad who stood up with a big smile and stuck out his hand.

"Good morning Inspector," he said, "I'm Brad Milton. I own the Cessna 182 out there and these are my documents."

Kennedy accepted the handshake. As soon as he saw the different log book, he knew Brad was from the United States.

"You're one of our American friends," he said with a smile. "It's okay, you don't have to show me your documents."

Brad's smile dropped like a rock.

"You're kidding, I hope. I've been waiting a long time for this moment." He hadn't let go of Kennedy's handshake.

"I'm sure the government monitors documents in the United States. I'll leave it to them," the inspector said, trying to reclaim his hand from the disappointed salesman.

Brad wasn't giving up. "I've been maintaining these documents for over ten years and I'd appreciate it if you would read them."

"Oh, it's not necessary," Kennedy said.

"Perhaps you don't understand," Brad replied. His tone sounded more persistent.

"I've been faithfully entering Time Out, Time Up, Time Down, Time In, Total Air Time and Total Flight Time for every flight. The airplane doesn't fly any better, but I do it because some government official might want to see the entries. Now you're here." He held onto Kennedy with one hand and reached for his log book with the other.

The inspector smiled weakly and accepted the book. Brad let go. Kennedy thumbed through a couple of pages and handed the log back. "Looks fine to me," he said tentatively.

"And how about the documents?" Brad asked scooping up the pile from the coffee table.

"Good, they look fine." Kennedy was sounding desperate.

"Can I show you the aircraft?" he asked.

"No, no, that won't be necessary," the inspector replied. He tried to back away.

Brad took him by the arm. "I insist. I never fly with passengers, but I've installed the government mandated 'Exit' signs over both door handles and those cute placards on the instrument panel that declare that flying a Cessna can be hazardous to your health. You'll be the first to see them."

Kennedy dutifully allowed Brad to escort him out the door. I watched while the inspector took a quick look inside the 182 and then hopped into his van and drove off.

Brad came back into the lounge wearing a big smile. "I've wanted that to happen for a long time," he said. "I feel so good, I might go up the road and join Muldoone and the boys for a beer!"

Chapter Thirty-two

Compass rose

Skid Sycamore was a Derry area aircraft broker. His activities didn't generate direct revenue for the flying school but Irving Mingy tolerated him anyway. The air service owner recognized that aircraft sales helped sustain business. Flying school customers who bought airplanes needed to store them, get them fixed and buy fuel. They were also likely to take more lessons, so Mingy allowed Skid to use our lounge as his Derry base of operations.

Skid was likable but slick. He was always trying to impress the men and embarrass the women with a new dirty joke. He was the right guy to invite to a cocktail party but the wrong one to be near your daughter.

There was a story circulating about Skid's days in the Air Force as a teenager. He learned to fly T-6 Harvards. Skid was out on a solo navigation flight one day when he was reported low flying down the main street of a nearby town. He was buzzing a girlfriend who worked in the restaurant. Someone in a second floor apartment read his tail numbers at eye level. Skid was told to report to the commanding officer when he landed back at the base.

The CO asked Skid if he had been the pilot low flying down the main street of the town.

"Yes, sir," Skid replied. "I was lost, sir. I was trying to read the name on the front of the post office."

"Well, Sycamore, did you have to do it in formation with your wingman?"

"Yes sir. He was lost too sir."

Skid came into Derry Air one day when a thick fog blanketed the airport. Localized fog was a regular at Derry when an east wind pushed moisture off Lake Ontario. The surrounding area could be clear.

I was ground briefing with Melville Passmore. Otherwise the lounge was empty. I heard Skid tell Angel that he needed an airplane to fly to Toronto to pick up someone. It was a typical

Skid operation. He was running behind. He had left it too late to make the two-hour drive to Toronto. He usually had a brokered aircraft at the Derry Airport that he could use on the pretense of a demonstration, but not this time.

Angel knew that I was nearly finished with Melville.

"We have an airplane, but you'll have to take an instructor," she told Skid.

"An instructor? What the Sam Hill for?" Skid exclaimed.

"You're not current," Angel replied. "Our rental policy requires an annual flight check with an instructor and you haven't had it. You can do it on the way."

Angel knew that Skid had thousands of flying hours in everything from Cubs to Learjets, but to her he was a freeloader who should be dinged for a dollar every chance she could get. This was a chance.

He took a big breath as if he was going to complain but he changed his mind. He knew Angel's word was law at Derry Air.

"I'll file a flight plan. What airplane is it?"

"Tango Victor Hotel."

Skid picked up the direct line telephone to the control tower. I finished with Melville and gave Angel our briefing time so she could write up a bill.

"You're going to fly to Toronto with Mr. Sycamore," Angel said.

"Okay," I said automatically but I had mixed feelings about the idea. I was going to be checking out one of the most experienced pilots on the airport in instrument flight rules weather. I was sure there was nothing I could teach the man but I knew that the IFR experience would be useful to me. It was a bonus that I was going to be paid for my time.

Listening to Skid's flight plan filing on the telephone was a good preview of the flight to come.

"An IFR flight plan to Toronto in Tango Victor Hotel, one of those Cherokees, full fuel, leaving in five minutes and you got all that other good stuff on file."

"Routing? Direct, is there another way? Time enroute? How long does it take to fly to Toronto in any airplane? Twenty minutes. The pilot is Sycamore."

He held the receiver toward Angel. "Talk to this guy," he said. "He's asking questions and I don't have time." He plunked the phone on the counter and fled out the door. I picked up the log book and followed.

Skid jumped into the airplane without a walkaround inspection and began pushing buttons. He got the engine running while I was still climbing into the right front seat. Skid released the brakes while I closed the door. He called ground control; I dug for my seat belt.

"Derry ground, this is TVH on an IFR to Toronto."

In the space of two minutes, Skid had broken every rule about preparing for a flight. I should have climbed back out of the airplane but I was too keen to focus on the risk. We were about to launch into a blanket of fog in a flying school hack of an airplane without a weather briefing, flight planning, charts or a checklist. TVH was equipped for basic instrument flight training but there was no duplication of equipment usually found on aircraft flown in actual bad weather.

"Tango Victor Hotel," the ground controller said. I recognized Diana's voice. "Be advised that the Derry Airport is below IFR departure limits with an indefinite ceiling of zero feet and one-eighth of a mile visibility in fog. Say your intentions."

I figured that was it. The flight was scrubbed and it wasn't such a bad idea. I hadn't counted on Skid's resourcefulness.

"Derry ground, TVH, we'll, ah, we'd like to taxi out to the compass rose on Echo Taxiway and check our deviation since we have the airplane up and running."

The compass rose was a circle of lines representing the points of the compass radiating from a centre. It was painted on the tarmac for aircraft mechanics to calibrate compasses.

There was a pause while Diana thought about Skid's sudden change from a flight request to a maintenance check. "Ah, Tango Victor Hotel is cleared all the way to Echo Taxiway for a compass swing.

"TVH."

Echo Taxiway intersected Runway 06 so Skid headed in that direction.

"This'll work out fine," Skid said in answer to my puzzled look. "The airport is closed, so we can sneak out without bothering anyone."

When he came to the runway, Skid taxied the Cherokee onto the centreline and hit full power. I had the same sinking feeling that you would have as a passenger in a car being chased by a police cruiser when the driver says, "I'll bet we can lose him."

I didn't know whether I was going to die or just get in a

whole lot of trouble.

All visual reference out the window disappeared when Skid rotated the airplane off the runway. I watched the flight instruments like a hawk. I wanted to know when we were going to crash.

As far as I could tell, Skid was flying the airplane quite well. It only took him a few seconds of overcontrolling to figure out that a wings level climb on TVH's well worn artificial horizon instrument came at a five degree left bank indication. Skid set up the radio navigation frequency for the approach track on Runway 06 and flew it away from the airport toward Toronto.

The control tower at Derry did not have radar but Skid kept the transponder turned off.

"I don't want Toronto radar to see us until we get a little ways from Derry," Skid offered.

Our communication radio was still tuned to the Derry ground frequency. "Tango Victor Hotel, are you at the compass rose yet?" Diana asked.

"Affirm," Skid replied.

"Call when you want to return."

"Rog."

"I have to keep my transmission short," Skid said to me, "otherwise their direction monitoring equipment will lock on us and they'll know we're not at the compass rose."

I nodded meekly. I knew we were going to get caught and technically I was pilot-in-command of this flight.

As we climbed through 1,500 feet, the sky brightened and we flew out of the fog into the clear. Skid continued the climb to 2,500 feet. He switched frequencies and called Toronto Terminal Control.

"Toronto, TVH is a Cherokee 30 miles southwest inbound for a landing at the International."

"Tango Victor Hotel, Toronto," the terminal controller replied, "squawk ident on 1200."

Skid punched the "ident" button on the radar transponder. I reached up and turned it on. Skid nodded.

"Tango Victor Hotel, Toronto, negative contact. Do you have a transponder?"

Always the jokester, Skid replied, "Hey, with this outfit, you're lucky we got a radio. I could be talking through a soup can tied to a string. Just a minute and I'll turn on the rotating beacon. Maybe you'll see us better."

Skid laughed and winked knowingly at me.

"Radar contact, Tango Victor Hotel, plan a straight in for Runway 06 Left. Call four miles on final."

We approached Toronto and landed without further incident. Skid turned off the runway, called ground control and received taxi instructions to the general aviation side of the airport. Then he shut off the master switch which killed all the electrics in the airplane except the engine ignition.

In answer to my questioning look, Skid said, "Mingy has the rental hour meter set in these airplanes to turn on and off with oil pressure, but they're run by the electric system. I won't have to pay for our taxi time with the master switch off."

Skid's passenger was waiting for us at one of Toronto's general aviation fixed base operators. It was his son. He had flown into Toronto on the airlines from university. He folded himself into the jump seats in the back of the Cherokee and promptly fell asleep. Skid asked Toronto ground control for taxi instructions for a VFR flight to Burlington.

"Burlington was in the clear when we flew in," he explained to me.

Now Skid was making sense. We could park the airplane at Burlington's airport and arrange for someone to pick us up by car. Maybe we could convince Diana that the airplane was in the Derry Air hangar and we had forgotten to call for instructions from Echo Taxiway.

"Do you know someone who can drive us from Burlington?" I asked hopefully.

"No. We're going over Burlington on our way to Hamilton."

"But Hamilton is probably still closed," I protested.

"I hope so," Skid answered with a grin. "If it's not, we're in trouble for not being at the compass rose."

I decided we were in trouble either way. If the fog had lifted, the controllers would know we were not there. If the weather was still below limits, we were going to die trying to land.

By now, Skid had the Cherokee airborne off Toronto's Runway 06L. It hadn't taken him long. He hadn't done any checks before takeoff. He banked left and headed southwest. Once he was clear of the Toronto Terminal Control airspace, he tuned in Hamilton Ground Control. There was no activity on the frequency. Over Burlington's uncontrolled airport, Skid turned off the radar transponder.

"That's so Toronto thinks we landed here."

Up ahead, we could see the blanket of fog streaming off Lake

Ontario. Skid set the radio navigation receiver to the approach frequency for Hamilton's Runway 06. Then he turned to a heading to intercept the runway centreline localizer and started a descent without reducing engine power.

"We'll fly a Backcourse Approach to Runway 24," he explained.

I had been doing this stuff with Henry in the Twin Comanche so I knew Skid was going to fly the centreline indicator for Runway 06 backwards to find the centreline for Runway 24. This was a standard practice in instrument flying but it was considered a non-precision type of approach. There was no radio altitude information so the approach was not supposed to be used when the clouds were below 500 feet or the visibility below one and a half miles.

Skid was descending through 2,000 feet above sea level according to the altimeter. The ground around the Derry Airport was at 800 feet above sea level. We were still flying in the clear with a solid blanket of fog below. I didn't know of any way for us to accurately determine when we had descended to the runway without seeing it first.

Skid commented as if he had heard my unasked question. "The shack for the localizer transmitter for Runway 06 is beside the end of Runway 24. When we pass it the needle will wiggle; that's when we'll dive for the runway."

Our indicated airspeed in Skid's power on descent was 120 knots. With the tailwind, we were flying 20 knots faster over the ground. The extra speed was going to make staying on the centreline more difficult. All of these things were running through my head unsaid as we descended into the fog at 1,500 feet above sea level.

When I flew the Backcourse Approach to Runway 24 with Henry, the centreline needle would swing nervously as we got close to the airport. I'd chase it in ever increasing oscillations until it went off the scale left or right. Henry would laugh and tell me to keep practising.

With Skid flying, the indicator stayed in the centre. The needle never moved more than its own hairline width. I thought it must have been broken but the failure flag was not showing. Skid's movements of the controls were nearly invisible.

We descended through 1,100 feet and then 1,000 feet. The power was still on and our speed was pegged at 120 knots. At 900 feet above sea level, we were about 100 feet above the ground and still flying in the soup. I couldn't see anything but fog. The localizer needle twitched. Skid chopped the engine power to idle and slowly eased back on the control wheel. At 800 feet on the altimeter, I couldn't see the runway, but the fog darkened as if the ground was near. Skid was still concentrating on the instruments. He pulled the aircraft's nose into level flight. As our speed bled off, the Cherokee slowly sank. Suddenly I could see the runway centreline. It looked like it was coming right into the windshield. I was about to shout, "runway contact", when the main tires kissed the asphalt.

The visibility had dropped since we had left. I could only see two of the centreline dashes ahead which was about 300 feet. Skid was steering down the runway still using the aircraft instruments. He gently applied the brakes and picked up the microphone. "TVH requests taxi clearance back to the ramp."

"Tango Victor Hotel is cleared Echo, Runway 06 to the ramp," the controller replied. It was Diana.

"TVH."

"Victor Hotel, did you get the compass swung okay?" she asked.

"Affirmative," Skid replied, "Thank you very much."

"Where were you when I called twenty minutes ago?"

"Ah, we must have had the volume turned down," Skid said. "Sorry about that." He flashed me a smile. "Was there a problem, tower?"

"No problem for me," Diana said. "I just wanted to tell you that the compass rose hasn't been on Echo since they repaved that taxiway last year."

Chapter Thirty-three

Dead head

Three black limousines rolled cautiously onto the Derry Air ramp. They stopped in a half circle around the flying school's Cessna 172. Irving Mingy stood solemnly beside the airplane with Eric Daedalus. The car doors opened and a dozen passengers stepped out. They were older people wearing funeral clothes and faces. One was carrying an urn.

This was to be the last flight of Robert Murdock. Murdock had been the flamboyant, popular and now departed mayor of Derry. The good food and stresses of the office had caught up with him. He had died of a heart attack following a ribbon-cutting ceremony for a new cocktail lounge in the city.

Murdock had been a strong promoter of Derry and its airport. His will had included the wish to be cremated along with the request that his ashes be spread over the city from an airplane.

The funeral home had called Derry Air. We had never done any "ash spreading" before. Manager Mingy quoted the funeral director $200, a tidy sum for what should have been a 20-minute flight. The director agreed.

Mingy had arranged for Daedalus to do the flight, which was why the two men were waiting on the ramp. They looked sharp. Instead of their usual open-necked shirts and rolled up sleeves, both men wore blue blazers, ties and grey pants. So far Eric had managed to control his perpetual grin and appeared appropriately reverend.

The arrangements called for the ashes, which were in the urn, to be handed over to the pilot while the former mayor's widow looked on. Daedalus would take the mayor on his last flight and only one of them would come back. He was supposed to sprinkle the ashes while flying across the city in sight of the airport and then return the empty urn to the widow.

The first part went as planned. The mayor's wife, accompanied by the funeral director, a few relatives, several city officials and a photographer from the *Derry Daily*, shook hands with Mingy and Daedalus. The chief flying instructor was presented with the urn which he dutifully placed in the right front seat. As an afterthought, he wrapped the seat belt around it. He climbed into the other side, started the engine and taxied out for takeoff. The airplane accelerated down the runway and lifted off, shallow and funeral-like. I watched from the flight lounge where I was waiting for a student. Daedalus positioned the Cessna at one end of the city and proceeded across. The flight looked normal except for a few wobbles, but when Daedalus turned, he headed back across the city instead of to the airport. The group of dignitaries stood patiently on the ramp while the Cessna recrossed the city three times. The mayor had been a big man, but it shouldn't have taken that long to dump his charred remains out the window.

The Cessna finally landed and taxied up to the group on the ramp. Daedalus climbed out. He looked different. He was no longer wearing a blazer or a tie. His hair had turned grey. He presented the mayor's widow with the urn. She and the other dignitaries climbed into the cars and left.

Daedalus hot-footed it into the office and headed straight for the coffee machine. I followed. I could see that his hair was covered in ashes.

"So what happened out there?" I asked.

Daedalus took a gulp of coffee before answering. "I guess the old guy didn't want to go," Daedalus said with a bit of a grin. "You know that airplane doesn't have an autopilot and never did fly straight. Well, I tried to steer with my knees while reaching for the urn and opening the window. Darcy had disconnected the arm on the left side window so it would open all the way up to the wing." Daedalus was laughing between sentences now.

"All I had to do was tip the urn at the window and let the slipstream suck old Murdock into oblivion. I should have practised with something else first. I found out that whatever gets sucked out of the front half of the window of a Cessna 172 gets blown in the back half. The mayor went sailing out the window all right and came in behind me. In the blink of an eye, he circled the cabin and landed on top of me. As quick as you can say Bob Murdock, I was covered in grey ash." Daedalus took a big gulp of coffee. "I can still taste him."

"I knew I couldn't go back to the airport and hand the widow the urn while wearing her husband, so I flew across town again. Have you ever tried to brush grey ash off a navy blue blazer?

Well it doesn't work. It smears. So I flew across town steering with my knees. I took the blazer and tie off. I figured the grey pants were okay."

"Yah, but you forgot about your hair," I said.

"Tell me about it," Daedalus continued. "So I landed back at the airport, stepped out of the airplane and handed the widow the urn. She said, 'Thank you young man. That must have been a hair raising experience for you.'"

"She was referring to the mayor in your hair, Eric."

"Oh no," he said, touching his head. He looked at the ashes on his fingers and then dove for the washroom, but not before Darcy saw him. The mechanic had come out of the shop to refasten the arm on the Cessna's window.

"Say, mean dandruff problem Eric. I didn't know you were a dead head."

Daedalus came out later looking washed and unsmeared. While we were finishing our coffee, the linecrew, Huey, Duey and Louey came into the lounge walking in single file. Huey was in the lead solemnly carrying a vacuum cleaner bag. They had just finished cleaning out the Cessna.

"Mayor Robert Murdoch at your disposal," Huey announced formally and the three of them broke into laughter.

The next day, the *Derry Daily* ran a picture of a grey-haired Daedalus handing back the urn to Mrs. Murdock. The caption read, "Mayor Murdoch comes to rest over the place he loved."

Chapter Thirty-four

Flight test

Henry and I had become good friends; too good. We joked around a lot and could be counted on to never give each other a straight answer.

Henry booked my Multi-Engine IFR flight test in the early fall.

"So you think I'm ready?" I asked.

"Well, if you're not, you'll fail," he replied matter of factly.

I had invested a lot of time and money that I couldn't afford into my instrument training.

"But you think I'll do all right?" I asked.

"The flight test is one way to find out," he said. He held his deadpan look.

"Well, if I'm marginal, let's do another lesson."

"You're marginal, but your flying's not bad." This time he cracked a smile.

"Thanks for nothing."

"You're welcome."

The instrument flight tests in our area were done by the government in Toronto, the busiest airport in Canada. The inspectors usually flew with the candidates to Derry for the tests because Toronto had too much traffic, but the Derry candidates still had to go there to pick them up.

Henry had arranged to fly his IFR renewal on the same day as my test. I knew this would make it easier for me, but I was still nervous. For the flight to Toronto, Henry put me in the left seat with the hood on and gave me a light lesson on the way. The activity distracted me into being less terrified. We were hoping that the inspector would test Henry first and let me ride in the back to watch. This would save money on the aircraft rental and give me a dry run.

When we walked into the instrument inspectors' office, my jaw dropped. We were greeted by my nemesis, Inspector Kennedy. Mr. Cold Fish himself had done every one of my annual instructor flight tests, making each one harder than the last. He never smiled or uttered an encouraging word. Most recently, he had conducted a ramp check at Derry Air, but it hadn't lasted long. Brad Milton had welcomed him so much that Kennedy felt obliged to leave. I don't think he had any warm feelings for me or Derry Air.

Normally inspectors in Kennedy's department didn't do IFR flight tests. All this was running through my head when I opened my mouth. "What are you doing here?" I blurted out.

Henry looked stricken. Kennedy's undertaker expression didn't change.

"I believe by these booking sheets," he said, "that you, I and Mr. Rains here are doing a flight test together this morning."

My mouth stayed open. Any of Henry's efforts to calm my nerves on the way to Toronto had been wiped out. I didn't know what to say.

Kennedy continued. "I'm here because the IFR department is short handed. I don't like doing instrument flight tests, so I would appreciate it if we could move along."

Henry recovered first. "We were wondering if we could ride together. I'll go first and we can switch seats at Derry. It'll save you time and us money."

"That is acceptable," Kennedy said and turned to the counter to sign himself out.

Henry leaned over and whispered in my ear. "It'll be fine. Close your mouth."

Henry asked Kennedy if he would like to see any flight planning.

"No, and don't show me a pre-flight inspection either. You made it here, so we'll leave straight away."

It was strange to meet a less than thorough Inspector Kennedy but I was beginning to feel better about my test.

Henry went first with Kennedy riding in the right seat and me in the back. We departed Toronto and flew directly to Derry. When we were getting close, Kennedy had Henry put the hood on and gave him simulated vectors for a straight-in Backcourse Approach to Runway 24. Henry was about to intercept the localizer six miles from the airport when Kennedy pulled the left engine power off and told him it was a simulated failure. It was absolutely the worst time to deal with a problem. I could feel my adrenaline pumping and I was just a passenger. Henry handled it well, skidding the airplane with rudder to bracket the centreline needle while going through the "engine failure on approach" check.

As we reached the minimum IFR altitude, Kennedy said, "This will be a missed approach. You are cleared to the Derry Beacon to hold southwest, maintain 3,000 feet."

Henry repeated the simulated clearance out loud and called the missed approach point. When he reached for the twin throttles to apply full power, Kennedy kept his hand on the left one.

"It's dead, remember?" he said.

It's nearly impossible to climb a Twin Comanche on one engine loaded with three big guys and lots of fuel on a warm day. The right engine climb is the worst because the main thrust comes from the outboard side of the propeller. The asymmetric thrust tries to roll the airplane upside down. The drag of the airplane crabbing through the air with the right rudder and aileron hanging out to counteract the roll kills the climb.

I could see that Henry had pegged the airspeed at the best single-engine rate of climb speed. He continued to fly the runway centreline needle toward the Derry Beacon. The rate of climb indicator showed one needle width above zero, about 150 feet per minute up. The right engine was howling at full power, the propeller was at full fine pitch and the landing gear and flaps were retracted. There was nothing else Henry could do to make the airplane climb better.

"Call reaching 3,000 feet," Kennedy said. He was trying to sucker Henry into raising the nose on the Comanche which would only reduce the speed and the climb. It would also result in a flight test failure.

Henry didn't buy it. He held on to 90 knots and informed Kennedy, who was acting as his air traffic controller, "Be advised that I will be entering the hold below 3,000 feet."

"I'm giving you the left engine back now," Kennedy said, "advise level at 3,000 feet and advise entering the hold."

Henry read back the requests. From behind, I could see the sweat trickling down the back of his neck, but he was flying the airplane beautifully.

As soon as Kennedy restored the power to the left engine, he turned off both of the VHF navigation receivers. Henry saw the warning flags on the indicators pop up and advised the "air traffic controller" of his equipment failures. Kennedy acknowledged.

Henry reached 3,000 feet while entering the hold. Kennedy turned the VHF receivers back on and cleared him for an ILS approach to Runway 06. Henry read the clearance back. Kennedy asked him to pretend that the right engine was on fire. Henry completed the fire drill which included shutting down the right engine and simulating a MAYDAY on the radio. He set up a descent for the approach.

Kennedy was working Henry hard. The atmosphere in the cockpit was tense. My hands were sore from gripping the seats. The inspector kept the pressure on by asking Henry what he would do if the right engine was still burning and the weather had gone below minimums for landing at Derry. Henry replied that he would continue the approach and drive the airplane onto Runway 06 even if he could not see it. Kennedy told him to pretend that this was the case.

The emergency had been timed so we were approaching the Derry Beacon four miles off the beginning of Runway 06 still 1,000 feet above the glide path. I would have gone around the hold pattern once to descend, but we were supposed to be on fire. Henry cut the power on his remaining engine, extended the landing gear and flaps and stuffed the Comanche's nose down so steeply that I was momentarily floating against my seat belt. Kennedy held his hand against the aircraft's ceiling to prevent him from bumping his head. Trying to capture the sensitive glide path indicator in a descent that steep is very difficult. I would have never tried it.

Henry called by the beacon inbound. Kennedy cleared him to land and told him to take the hood off at 100 feet above ground. Henry had obviously practised this approach enough to know the various glide path altitudes inside the beacon. With the indicator still pegged below us, Henry knew when to reduce his descent by our altitude. The needle still came in fast. He hauled back on the control wheel, pressing us in our seats. The airplane porpoised while he fought to hold the glide path. He added power to the left engine which swung us right. He kicked the rudder and recaptured the centreline. It wasn't pretty, but he held the needles to 100 feet, took the hood off, cut the power and landed.

I was sweating just watching. There was no way I could have flown those situations as well as Henry. I resigned myself to the fact that I was going to fail my test and felt better for it. I could chalk the flight up to a good practice session and hope for a different inspector next time.

Kennedy directed Henry to pull onto a taxiway and told the air traffic controller that we would be shutting down long enough to switch pilots. He said nothing to acknowledge Henry's performance one way or the other.

The inspector and Henry climbed out of the airplane and I hopped into the pilot's seat. When they got back in, I took my time going through the start checklist. Henry had taught me to be slow and deliberate. Kennedy looked at his watch. "We've been through all that," he said. "Just start up and get going."

It bugged me that he would pressure me like that but I just took a deep breath and continued with the checks with all the pedantic uncertainty of a student pilot. I figured as soon as I rushed that I'd miss something and the test would be over. Kennedy drummed his fingers on the glare shield and huffed audibly. I started the engines and then proceeded to slowly test the avionics one at a time.

"We don't need to do that," Kennedy barked impatiently. "Assume they all work. I have a clearance for you when you're ready to copy."

My heart was pounding from nervousness, but I decided to stick to my guns. "I'm not ready," I said.

"Well, you'd better get ready," Kennedy said with more steel in his voice. "I'm not waiting all day."

I stopped what I was doing, turned and looked him in the eye. I was shaking but his attitude was strengthening my resolve.

"I'm pilot-in-command of this flight," I said in a wavy voice. "I'm going to do the checks. You can wait or walk back to Toronto."

I was sorry that I'd said it as soon as I had spoken. I could feel my face turning beet red. I waited for his explosion.

Kennedy actually smiled. "Okay, Mr. Commercial Pilot," he said calmly. "I'll wait. Let me know when you're ready."

He had been bluffing his impatience to catch me off guard. The thought of it made me angry, but I bit my tongue and decided to quit talking while I was ahead.

I did my checks and told him I was ready. He gave me a clearance to depart Runway 06 into a hold inbound on the Backcourse Approach to Runway 24. His tone was deliberately slow.

It was an exercise that I had done many times with Henry. I read the clearance back, took off and entered the hold. Once I was well established in the pattern, Kennedy simulated a right engine failure. When I had finished securing it, I pretended to radio a MAYDAY and requested an approach. He cleared me for the Backcourse for Runway 24. I flew the procedure. It was ropy but acceptable.

Kennedy advised me on final that I could expect a missed approach. On the overshoot, he restored power to the right engine and then shut off the VHF receivers. He cleared me for an NDB Approach to Runway 06. I acknowledged the equipment failures, read back the clearance and flew the approach. Kennedy didn't say or do anything until I was on final for the runway.

"At the missed approach point, do an overshoot," he said. "I'll have a clearance for you to Toronto."

I flew the overshoot and told him I was ready to copy. He gave me a clearance direct to Toronto at 3,000 feet. So far Kennedy had been easy on me compared to what he had done with Henry but I didn't complain. I realized that I might pass this test with one more acceptable approach at Toronto.

After I had leveled off at 3,000 feet, Kennedy asked me what I would do if only two green lights came on when I selected the landing gear down. I gave him a rehearsed spiel about recycling the gear up and down, checking the circuit breaker and the light bulb on the one that was out.

"What if the light bulb is dead?" he asked.

"Then I replace it with one of the illuminated bulbs."

"That isn't necessary," he said. "There are other replacement bulbs in this airplane. Do you know where?"

I was stumped on that one. I knew there weren't any spare bulbs with the fuses or in the glove box.

"No, sir," I replied. I was still flying under the hood.

Kennedy reached up to the top of the instrument panel, unscrewed the inner marker light and dropped the bulb from it into his hand. He stuck his hand under my face. "This is the same bulb," he said.

"That's good to know," I replied lamely. I didn't know what else I could say. I hoped my lack of bulb knowledge was not grounds for a failure. It seemed to make him happy to teach me something.

Next he gave me simulated radar vectors to intercept the straight-in approach to Runway 06 Left at Toronto. "When you reach minimums, take the hood off and land," he said.

"Yes sir," I replied.

When the localizer needle started to move toward the centre, I turned to intercept the runway centreline. In the turn, Kennedy pulled the power back on one engine.

"Simulated engine failure," he announced.

I launched into the engine failure check. "Mixture, pitch, power," I called out, "gear up, flaps up, dead foot, dead engine," I said. I struggled to keep the airplane straight on the localizer with the left rudder. "The right engine is dead," I declared.

At that point I was supposed to reach for the right throttle and pull it toward idle to verify that the right engine was dead. This was easy since Kennedy would have pulled the right throttle back to simulate the failure.

My brain faded and I grabbed the left throttle. "Verifying the right engine," I called out.

With that, the airplane went dead quiet as I pulled the power off the only operating engine. The next thing I heard was the crack of Henry's head hitting the ceiling in the back. He had fallen asleep after his high-pressure flight test. The sudden silence woke him up with a start. He had bolted upright and cracked his head.

I rammed the left throttle open, grabbed the other one and announced, "Verifying the right engine!"

I knew that was it. You don't pull the wrong engine on a flight test, if only for a second, and pass. I continued on the approach but I knew I was flying for pride now. I nailed the localizer and captured the glide path for Runway 06 Left. I simulated a MAYDAY call and asked for the crash equipment to be available beside the runway. Kennedy said, "Roger, the equipment is standing by. You are cleared to land Runway 06 Left."

"Cleared to land on six left," I replied.

I held the needles to the missed approach point, took the hood off, extended the undercarriage and landed.

I felt like crying after riding such an emotional roller coaster for an hour and then failing the test. Kennedy said nothing as I taxied onto the ramp. When I shut down, he said, "Come on in and we'll do the paperwork."

Henry and I exchanged unknowing glances as we followed him to the office.

"First I'll need some money from you for the flight tests and endorsements," he said.

The word "endorsements" meant a pass for both of us. I couldn't believe it. I looked at Henry. He shrugged.

"Are you suggesting that we both passed?" I asked Kennedy.

He looked up from his paperwork. "Don't you think Mr. Rains did a good job?"

"Yes sir, but I thought I failed when I pulled the power off the good engine."

"No," he replied. "That's why we have the verification on the checklist. You just proved it worked.

"Here's an Instrument Endorsement valid for six months," he said, handing me a card. "I hope I'm not still doing IFR flight tests when you return, but if I am, I'll expect you to be able to fly like Mr. Rains."

He handed Henry his card.

"Good day gentlemen."

"Good day, sir," we said.

We bumped into each other trying to get through the door before Kennedy changed his mind. We speed-walked across the ramp. I was about to break into a run when Henry stopped. He screwed up his face into a stern look and said in a low voice, "When you return, I'll expect you to be able to fly like Mr. Rains." Then he doubled over laughing.

"Ya, but when he said, 'Good day gentlemen,' he was looking at me."

"You. You're going to fly left seat home and you can expect a simulated engine failure at any time!"

"Can you stay awake long enough?"

"Ha. Listen to you, glider pilot. I'll never fall sleep in an airplane with you again!"

"I don't care. I've got an Instrument Rating."

Chapter Thirty-five

Glider

I charged into the house that night. "I passed, I passed, I passed!" I yelled. I grabbed Susan, hugged her and spun her around.

"That's great, Honey," she said. She gave me a big smile.

I launched into a staccato description of my day. "We had old stone-faced Kennedy for an inspector. He tried to hurry me into making a mistake, but I told him to hold his horses. I was nervous but it worked. He backed off."

"Good for you, Honey," she said, still giving me a wide smile.

I told Susan how Henry had cracked his head on the ceiling when I had pulled the wrong throttle and then called me a glider pilot. She listened patiently while I explained how I had aced the last approach even though I thought I had failed. Then I told her how Henry's ride had been harder and how he had handled it.

"Good for both of you," she grinned.

When I finally calmed down a bit, she started to make dinner. As I started to relax, I realized three things: Susan was cooking steak instead of macaroni and cheese; she had called me "Honey" at least twice; and she was wearing one of those I-know-more-than-you smiles.

"What's happening with you?" I asked.

She looked at me sideways and saw that I had recovered from my excitement enough to notice the smiles and steaks.

"I have good news too," she announced.

"Tell me," I replied.

"I've been promoted again. You're now looking at the new manager of the East End Mall branch of the Fashion and Designer Emporium."

"That's fantastic!" I exclaimed.

We had another round of hugs.

"Tell me more."

"Well, it was quite unexpected. Norbert Bronze, the owner of the chain, came into the store from Toronto. I had never seen him before so I didn't know who he was. It was a great opportunity to put both feet in my mouth but I didn't. I was the only one on the floor so I asked if I could help him. He said, 'I've been hearing good things about you.' I thought he meant the store, so I told him that we had the best ladies wear company in the business. I laid it on really thick and then asked if he was shopping for someone special.

"'No,' he said, 'I'm Norbert Bronze and I came here to interview you. You've been recommended for the manager's job at East End Mall. I think the interview is over. The job's yours if you want it.'"

"That's great. Congratulations! When do you start?"

"Monday morning."

"Super! I'm really proud of you. I'm sorry I barged in and monopolized the conversation with my flight test."

"That's okay," she said. "I'm glad you passed. Now we won't need to spend so much money on your training."

"Right. The Instrument Rating is valid for six months and now I can stay current by teaching other instrument students."

"And with my raise in pay," Susan added, "things won't be so tight."

"Right."

I should have been looking at her during that last exchange, but I wasn't.

We enjoyed our steak and potatoes. Lady drooled until we gave her a piece. We were all feeling very "up scale".

After supper, Susan quietly said, "What do you think of my teaching riding in the evenings and on days off when you're working?"

"Sure," I said. "Where?"

"Here," she replied.

"Here? We don't have the horses or the facilities."

She put on the sly smile again. "Not yet," she said. "I thought you might have time now to build more stalls."

"How many more?"

"Well, I talked to Hans and Gertrude. They board their horses near Derry but would be willing to let me use them for lessons in exchange for board here."

I had met Hans and Gertrude through Susan. They were a perfect couple. He was a know-it-all and she agreed with everything that he said. They lived nearby. Susan had already tested my tolerance of them by inviting them for dinner. It hadn't been good.

132

The look on Susan's face told me that she wasn't finished. "And?"

"And the neighbours up the road have a pony we can use."

"So that's three new stalls?" I asked.

"Four," she replied. The smile this time was a guilty one.

"Gertrude told me about a young horse at the Derry stable that was going to be sold for meat. I bought him on the way home tonight for $50." She blushed as she spoke.

"You've been busy."

"I know. I would've talked to you about the new horse first, but he was going to the auction tomorrow."

"What were you going to do if I had failed the flight test?"

"Oh, I knew you'd make it."

"You wouldn't have been that confident if you had been there."

"The horse is really gentle," Susan said, changing the subject. "He's perfect for beginning riders. I have everything I need to teach riding except the stalls. Hans said he'd help you build them," she added hopefully.

I had no good reason to object to the riding instructor idea but I drew the line at Hans. "The Windy Acres Riding Academy, yes; the Hopeless Hans Construction Company, no."

"But winter's coming. You're going to need help."

"Help, yes; Hans no. I'll find someone."

"Okay," she said, giving me a hug. "Glider comes this weekend."

"Glider?"

"Yes, the horse I bought today. He didn't have a name until now."

Chapter Thirty-six

A guy can't win

The next day the weather was bad. Henry related my power lever goof over coffee with any Derry Air staff who would listen. I told them about Henry cracking his head from a sound sleep.

Later, I mentioned Susan's riding instructor idea to Henry.

"The only hitch is getting four stalls built in the barn before the snow flies," I said.

"No problem. You should be able to knock those together in no time."

"You're talking to a man with two left thumbs and no power tools."

Henry's face lit up. "I'll give you a hand. I paid for my Commercial Pilot Licence by working for my father-in-law's construction company."

I knew that Henry was handy but he was a busy family man. I hadn't mentioned the barn to solicit his help.

"You work too much as it is," I said without meaning it. "You need to spend more time with Leanne and the kids."

"That's a great idea," he said.

He had lost me. "What's a great idea?" I asked.

"I'll bring the family to your place. Susan can give Gretchen and Victor riding lessons while you and I build stalls. What do you say?"

I liked it. Henry and I could have fun working in the barn while Susan tested her desire to be a riding instructor on Vicious and Greedy.

"Are you sure?" I asked.

"I'm good for it if Susan is."

"Okay, we'll take you up on it if you don't fall asleep during construction work."

"Hey, you beggars can't be choosers. Let's check the booking sheets."

Angel helped us to arrange a day off together on a Sunday. We were doing that when Ray Tragunno came into the flying school for coffee. Now that I had my Instrument Rating, I was anxious to talk to him about the life of an airline pilot.

"Did I ever tell you what my wife said after my first flight on the 747?" Ray asked.

"No," Henry and I chorused. Ray always told a good story on himself.

"It was to London Heathrow," he said. "I'd never been there. We flew over starting on a Monday and arrived on a Tuesday. During the layover, I did some sightseeing, had a couple of meals with the rest of the crew and flew back. When I got home, Elsie asked me if I'd had a good time. 'Sure,' I said.

"Well, she lit into me something fierce. She called me all sorts of names like 'no good' and 'two timer'. Apparently the whole time I was in training she'd worried that I'd ride off into the sunset with an airplane load of stews and party my way to Europe and back."

Henry and I looked at each other. Neither of us had considered what our wives thought of airline pilots. Susan and Leanne were both capable of reacting like Ray's wife.

"So the next week," Ray continued, "I was scheduled for the same trip. When I got back, Elsie asks if I had a good time. 'No,' I said. Then she calls me a 'No good, bold-faced liar', among other things. A guy can't win. I tried bringing her back little gifts from overseas but she accused me of trying to buy her off. I sent her a card from London once. She said that I must have been feeling guilty about something because I had never sent her a card before."

"How long did this go on?" Henry asked.

"Oh, forever. She's still mad every time I come home from a trip. I don't say or do anything no matter what she asks. By the third day, she is fine, but then I have to fly again."

Ray had started flying for the airline as a second officer, the third pilot in the cockpit. He sat sideways behind the other two pilots and acted as a flight engineer.

"How long do you have before you make co-pilot," I asked.

"Oh, about five or six years," he said. "I'm looking forward to it. I'll be flying the short hauls without layovers. Maybe Elsie will sleep with me again."

We laughed only because Ray laughed. He was lucky that he thought it was funny.

"Of course," he added, "when I get promoted, I'll have to see you guys to get my Instrument Rating back."

"You mean, the airline doesn't provide you with proficiency training?" I couldn't believe it.

"Not as a pilot. I work as a flight engineer. I let my IFR Rating lapse last year. If they don't want to pay for it, neither do I."

"That's okay," Henry said. "You don't have to do flight tests with stone-faced Kennedy like we had to yesterday."

He related the "glider pilot story" to Ray.

"I'd 've failed you," Ray said with a laugh. "He probably didn't want to fly with you again."

"Nice guy," I replied. "Come on back for IFR training anytime. I'd be glad to make your life miserable."

Ray just chuckled.

The next Sunday, Henry and I built stalls in the calving section of the barn. He was good. I'd be standing there sizing things up and he'd just start cutting and hammering boards. The odd time he'd make a mistake. He'd toss the wood aside, pick up a new piece and say, "I love making firewood with other people's lumber."

By noon, we had four stalls roughed in.

I worried about Susan. It was one thing to give kids a riding lesson for an hour, but I didn't envy her trying to keep Vicious and Greedy busy for a whole day. It was a wasted worry. She had it all planned. She had the two kids cleaning tack, brushing the horses, hauling water and thanking her for it. Susan had the enthusiasm to hold their attention, not to mention the height and volume to make it stick.

The weather was one of the last warm days of the fall. At lunch we had a hot dog roast outside. When Susan finally let the kids ride, she put Victor on Sunny and Gretchen on Glider. The pair looked funny because Glider was only half of Sunny's size but neither horse would do more than walk, Sunny because he was too old and Glider because he had been undernourished as a colt. Susan was good about making the kids feel like accomplished riders.

During a pause in the afternoon, Henry mentioned that he was having second thoughts about joining the airlines.

"Because of what Ray said about his wife?" I asked, half joking.

"No," Henry said with a smile. "Leanne and I have talked about it and it wouldn't bother her. I've applied to more than one airline but I'm kind of glad they haven't called."

"Why's that? I thought you and I were destined for the big time."

"Well, don't let me hold you back," Henry said. He was smiling, but he sounded serious. "I like working with the students. I like the fun we have at Derry Air. I don't like the idea of being just another number flying sideways around the world at 35,000 feet."

"So why have you applied to the airlines?"

"I have a wife and two kids to support. The airlines offer money and security. Why are you applying?"

It was the first time anyone had asked me.

"I'm applying because you are. You and every other pilot I know."

"Well, you're a good instructor," Henry said. "You too might think again. Come on. Let's get back to work."

"Yes sir."

Chapter Thirty-seven

Moose

If you were asked to pick Moose out of a crowd, you'd have no trouble. Moose was a lumbering, six-and-a-half-foot tall, barrel-chested behemoth who created large areas of shade. He belonged to a motorcycle gang, drove a Harley Davidson and wore smelly black leather over a dirty T-shirt and jeans. His scarred face was a living history of misspent youth. His head was mostly bald except for a fringe of long hair which he covered with a German World War II helmet.

I wasn't there when Moose started his lessons at Derry Air but Henry had told me about it.

"The first day that he came into the flying school, I thought we were about to discover the missing link between man and the apes," Henry recalled with a laugh. "He walked through the door hunched over with his knuckles nearly dragging on the ground. When he spotted Angel, he ambled over to the counter and uttered one of the longest sentences of his life. 'I wanna learn how to fly.'

"Angel called me over and told me to give Moose an Introductory Flying Lesson. I introduced myself and the gorilla nearly broke my hand. He said his name was Moose, but without any front teeth, it came out as 'Moothe'. I didn't laugh. I didn't want my body rearranged. I outlined the flying lessons. Moose listened briefly and then pulled a huge roll of money from his dirty jeans pocket. He paid for the whole course in cash. I quickly said that the outline was the minimum time and that it might take more. It was possibly the smartest thing I have ever done. He plopped down another grand and asked Angel to tell him when it ran out.

"We went out to the flight line. Moose almost fit into a Piper Cherokee 140 with the seat rolled all the way back. 'I think the helmet has to come off, Moose,' I said. He didn't like the idea because it exposed his chrome dome, but he did as I asked.

"Moose turned out to be a good learner. What he lacks in smarts, he makes up for with motor skills. He told me that he had always wanted to fly and he had looked at a lot of aviation magazines. He understands everything as long as I relate to riding a motorcycle.

"During our lessons, the airplane flies permanently left wing low. Moose is never going to know what it is like to fly without holding right aileron, but he flies quite well, thank god. I might have dual controls but there is no question of my ever over-powering Moose.

"The only trouble we had was when Moose discovered that the Cherokee cruised at 100 mph. He was disappointed. He drives the Harley faster on his way to the airport. I quickly explained that the Cherokee was a training airplane and that other ones went much faster. 'Think of it as a Harley on training wheels,' I said. That seemed to satisfy him."

Moose liked Henry. It was an indication of what a great people-person Henry was. At the end of a lesson, the two could be seen debriefing in the lounge. Moose listened to Henry's every word. When they were done, Moose gave Henry a big toothless grin and said, "Okay, boss," which came out, "Okay, bothe."

Henry milked the friendship in Moose's absence. When a Derry Air staff said something sarcastic to Henry, he'd reply, "I'll have to call Moose. He'll be waiting at your house to straighten you out, literally."

The most exciting Saturday in the history of Derry Air was the day that Moose showed up with his gang. About 80 of Satan's finest rode their motorcycles past the parking lot, around the hangar and onto the ramp. They parked the bikes in front of the lounge. They were in various stages of chop. Some had sidecars and many had a passenger on the back. They all followed Moose into the flying school lounge. The place filled with tattooed bikers in black leathers. All conversation and activity in the lounge stopped.

Moose walked over to where Henry was briefing a student. "I juth want ya to meet the gang," he said. "Guyth, thith is my inthructor, Henry."

Most of the "guys" said, "Hi." Some clapped slowly. Then they wandered around the lounge looking at the pictures on the walls. A couple of them gave Angel a big smile. I had taken refuge behind the flight desk next to her. Moose gave me a nod and headed for the door. The rest of the gang followed. They fired up their bikes and were off with a squeal of tires and the roar of open exhaust.

The three or four staff in the lounge looked at each other a bit stunned. The pictures were still on the walls, there were no vending machines missing and we were all still alive.

Chapter Thirty-eight

Derry 1 - Condor 1

The entrance to the Derry Airport was guarded by a Harvard on a cement pedestal. The big yellow military training airplane had been perched in front of the Airport Legion Hall since the 1950s. It stood, or more accurately, pivoted, as a tribute to the airport's beginning as a training base during World War II. It also acted as a giant weather vane. Volunteers from the local air museum had mounted it on a post and bearing plate so it could swing into the wind.

The Harvard looked smart. The Legion Women's Auxiliary, aided by funding from the Air Force Association and the Imperial Order of the Daughters of the Empire, had recently arranged for it to be taken down and repainted. Derry Air had done the work. Irving Mingy had given the ladies a good price knowing he could get his money back in the publicity that surrounded such projects.

The guys in the shop had done a great job. They replaced all the windows, stripped off the old paint along with the generations of bird dirt and acid rain streaks. They applied several shiny coats of school-bus yellow. Mingy had the letters "DA" painted into the military registration. There was also discreet, but easy-to-read lettering on the fuselage under the tail: "This aircraft was refurbished by Derry Air."

Before the Harvard was hoisted back up, the good ladies of the Women's Auxiliary placed male mannequins in the front and back seats. They dressed the "pilots" in period military uniforms complete with leather helmets and headsets.

On the night of October 31, someone climbed up to the Harvard and opened the cockpit. They undressed both mannequins and left the clothes on the floor. Then they shoved the rear-seat pilot upside down in the front cockpit in a suggestive arrangement.

I noticed the pink pretzel of legs and arms in the Harvard when I drove into work the next morning. It was a gusty spring day. The airplane was swinging back and forth in the wind which helped animate the scene in the cockpit. I immediately assumed that this had been the work of Huey, Duey and Louey.

In the flying school, manager Mingy was yelling at the three linecrew in his office. The door was closed, but we could all hear. He told them that the prank would damage Derry Air's reputation and then ordered them to get out there and fix the mannequins.

Huey, Duey and Louey walked out, heads bowed and silent, followed by a red-faced Mingy. Eric Daedalus, walked over to him and pointed out that the three linecrew had worked the early shift the day before and were probably in a bar when the deed was being done last night.

"You're probably right," Mingy replied. "But there's no harm done. The dressing down will compensate for the next time they screw up and I'm not here."

Keith Harrison was my first student of the day. He had noticed the Harvard and wasn't too shy to mention it. "If you're giving lessons military style today," he said, "I'd rather fly with someone better looking." He laughed and then added, "I've heard of attitude and movement lessons, but that's too much."

Harrison and I went flying. Someone in the Derry Control Tower had obviously spotted the mannequins. When we called for taxi clearance for a local flight, the controller asked for our planned altitude.

"Four thousand," was our reply.

"Aren't you going for the mile high club?" the controller responded with a chuckle.

That would be the end of the story, except we found out that it was the Condor Aviation staff in the next hangar who had rearranged the mannequins. It was retaliation for the sign altering we had done to them on April 1st.

Someone tipped off the *Derry Daily*, the local newspaper. They dispatched a reporter who arrived while Duey and Louey were in the de-icing bucket fighting to get the tunics back on the mannequins. The reporter talked to Huey, who was in the truck. The story was printed as a caption under a picture of Louey adjusting the helmet on a mannequin. It was a big lie, which is what anyone would get from listening to Huey. It said that the Derry Air "maintenance crew" were doing their annual spruce-up of the Harvard, a service provided free-of-charge by the flying school. The coverage garnered positive feedback from our customers, the Legion Women's Auxiliary and the community.

Mingy was pleased. He had the linecrew prop a hand-painted plywood sign against our hangar facing the competition. It read,

"Derry 1, Condor 1".

Chapter Thirty-nine

JBI

Derry Airport manager Stan Westley was pleased as punch. The government had given him a James Brake Indicator. This was a metal box with an indicator scaled 0 to 1.0. It measured the stopping suitability of a surface such as a runway. On slippery days, the JBI reading was relayed to pilots to give them an idea of the runway conditions before they tried to land.

The James Brake box was usually mounted in an airport maintenance truck. In bad weather, the truck would be driven down the runway and the brakes applied. The JBI deceleration reading would be relayed to the control tower and weather office where inbound pilots could hear about it.

Westley's JBI arrived the same week as the first freezing rainstorm of the season. On Thursday morning everything in and around Derry was covered with a thick layer of ice. The Derry municipal crews did a good job of salting the roads. I drove to work on the Volkswagon's bald tires without too much trouble but I had difficulty getting from the parking lot to the lounge. The ice coating was hard and smooth. I felt like a day-old calf trying to walk.

Salting the airport asphalt was not an option because of the corrosion it caused in aircraft. Westley would normally have applied urea instead, a non-corrosive chemical fertilizer that works like salt, but the wind was too strong. Urea acts slowly and Westley knew that all the expensive fertilizer would be blown into the grass before it did any good. He would be left with an icy runway, a hole in his budget and the prospect of having to cut the grass twice as often in the spring.

Westley had one other option. The city maintained a hot sand pile. The pre-warmed granules melted into the ice to provide an abrasive surface. The cost of the heated sand was high. Before

144

Westley phoned the city to order it, he decided to test the braking on the runway.

He and his helper, Albert, had not yet installed the James Brake Indicator in the airport truck so Westley placed it on the passenger seat of his old Buick station wagon. He strapped it in with the seat belt so it would give a solid reading when he hit the brakes. He set off down the ice-covered taxiway toward Runway 06. The steering felt loose on the slippery surface, but the car slowed promptly when he applied the brakes. He received permission from the ground controller to proceed onto the runway. He accelerated to 50 mph. It was not Boeing 737 landing speed, but it was as fast as he dared in the Buick. He slammed on the brakes expecting to start an almighty slide. The old boat of a car slowed surprisingly well. It did slide, but Westley was stopped less than halfway down the 6,000-foot runway. He checked the JBI. The meter read "point 6", the equivalent for a wet runway, not ice covered.

Westley tried it again on the remaining runway and got the same reading. On the way back, he got braver and accelerated to 65 mph before hitting the brakes. The station wagon slewed somewhat but stopped with another "point 6" reading. Westley reported the JBI indication to the control tower and told them that he would not be ordering sand.

There were two scheduled airlines that flew into Derry. One serviced the east-west routes in Canada and the other flew south into the United States. Each carrier had a couple of flights in the morning and the evening.

The first inbound flight called commencing an approach. The cockpit crew confirmed that the JBI was "point 6". The airplane was a Boeing 737 out of Montreal. The captain on this airplane was faced with having to increase his approach speed to compensate for the 60 degree crosswind and its associated turbulence. That would extend his landing distance as would the anticipated "wet runway" deceleration of a "point 6" JBI. He was probably figuring on using about the first 4,000 feet of the 6,000-foot runway.

The weather was clear. The pilot reported the runway in sight well back on a visual approach. I was in the Derry Air lounge pouring my first coffee after my slide across the ramp. I could see Runway 06 out the lounge window but not the approach. I had heard the pilot call on the office monitor so I watched to see the airliner appear from the left.

The 737 came into view cocked in a left wing down, crosswind approach. The pilot nailed it on the runway left wheel first at the 1,000-foot mark. From there, the cockpit would have been a more exciting vantage point than mine. I guess the captain applied the brakes after the other main wheel had touched down but nothing happened. The ice covered runway provided almost no braking. He then pulled the two throttles into reverse thrust to help slow the airplane. As the speed reduced, the 737 acted like a giant weather vane and started to swing left into the crosswind. The captain pushed the right pedal. The rudder responded but the nose wheel did not. The swing to the left lessened, but the captain had to resort to less reverse thrust on the left engine. The staggered thrust straightened the airplane but it reduced the deceleration. The end of the runway was coming up fast. The captain pumped the brakes, but it didn't help. There was nothing more he could do but enjoy the slide.

I couldn't see the far end of the runway from the lounge so the drama of the moment was lost on me. The air traffic controllers saw it all from the tower. Diana Bates told me about it later.

"They had less than 20 feet of runway left when they stopped," she said. "They had passed the numbers and were well into the end marks at the beginning of Runway 24. I bet they had to change their underwear after that one!"

When he was finally stopped, the 737 captain called on the radio. "What was that JBI reading again?"

"Point six," Diana replied.

"It should be point zero six," the captain said. "There is no grip out here at all."

He sounded like he was trying hard to control his anger. When he started to turn the airliner around, the nosewheel slid sideways on the ice. He had to apply forward thrust on the right engine and reverse on the left. To taxi down the centre of the runway, the pilot had to crab the airliner into the wind by modulating different amounts of engine thrust. It was beautiful to watch. When he came to the intersection of Runway 12, he swung the airplane left with asymmetric thrust to continue taxiing to the terminal ramp. The 737 paraded past the front of the Derry Air flight lounge cocked well to the left.

The test of this pilot's skill was not over. He turned right onto the short taxiway that ran from Runway 12 to the ramp. The wind was now behind him and his airplane was pointed at the

146

terminal building. The wind pushed on the 737, increasing its taxi speed. The pilot hit the brakes. The mainwheels stopped turning but the airliner continued unabated. I could see the Derry Air linecrew, Huey, Duey and Louey waiting to unload the airplane with the train of baggage carts. The captain applied reverse thrust on both engines. The blast was strong enough to move the three baggage carts and the linecrew across the ice.

The captain was smart enough to realize that the airliner would not stay parked in those conditions with its tail to the wind, so he swung it around 180 degrees.

The mystery of the erroneous JBI reading was solved when Huey, Duey and Louey pointed out to Westley that his Buick was riding on studded snow tires.

Chapter Forty

Am I in London?

At 128 flying hours, Melville was Derry Air's leading marathon student pilot. At times, teaching him two lessons a week seemed to be my whole career, but Melville never wavered from his goal of a pilot licence so neither did I.

I picked a clear, low-traffic day during the week for his solo cross-country. It was supposed to be a three-legged, three-hour flight from Derry to the town of Pie, south of London, Ontario, to Kitchener and back. I checked his flight planning, asked him to phone Derry Air at each stop and signed him off. I was nervous but Eric backed me up.

"You had to send him sometime," the chief flying instructor said. "You've done everything necessary. He's as ready as he can be."

"Thanks Eric," I said. "I appreciate your confidence."

"No problem," he replied and then added. "If he crashes, don't worry, the airplane is insured. Hee, hee, hee."

I was in the Derry Air lounge when Melville made his first call.

"Hello," he said nervously. "Am I in London?"

"I don't know, Melville," I replied. "What happened to Pie?"

"I dunno, but the instructor here said it was London."

"Let me speak to him."

"Hi, this is Jethro. Your student is in Pie. We were just kidding when we welcomed him to London."

I could hear a stupid grin in his voice.

"You're flexing your sense of humour on the wrong student," I said. "I hope I can return the favour sometime. Now if you can convince him that he's in Pie, I'd appreciate your helping him on his way."

"Sure thing."

I was flying with a student when Melville called at his next stop. Eric told me that Melville had telephoned — from Sarnia.

"I'll go get him," I said.

"No," Eric replied firmly, "I asked the chief instructor there to gas up Melville's aircraft and to check over his flight planning for a leg straight back to Derry."

"But Sarnia is 90 degrees off course from Pie to Kitchener."

"It is, but apparently Melville map read his way to Sarnia and knew where he was the whole time. He had forgotten to reset his heading indicator and followed the correct heading 90 degrees off course."

Eric could tell that I wasn't happy with his decision.

"Look," he said, "Melville knows what he's doing and so does the CFI at Sarnia. If you go and get him now, he'll lose the confidence you have built up in him. You've done your job, now let him do his."

Melville proved Eric right. I was in the air again when Melville called the Derry Tower approaching the control zone. Diana was the controller. She cleared him to a right downwind to Runway 24.

"I'm goin' to fly over the farm first to show the folks I'm back," he replied.

"So near yet so far," I thought. "He'll probably crash buzzing his farm."

Before I could say anything on the frequency, Diana saved the day.

"That's not in your flight plan, Melville, so you can't do that. Call on the downwind to Runway 24."

"Okay, tower."

Chapter Forty-one

Splish, splash

Moose was in the flight lounge waiting for Henry.

"Hi, Moose," I said. "Henry is flying, but he'll be down in a minute."

One of his beefy arms rose and a finger the size of a fireplace log pointed outside. "Whath thath polith plane doin'?"

He had forgotten his false teeth again. He was pointing at our Cessna 172 with "POLICE" painted on the side. I scrambled to think of a response that wouldn't upset the sleepy giant. Moose had more muscle in his ears than I had in my whole body.

"It belongs to the police, Moose. They use it for highway patrol."

Derry Air owned the airplane. It was only a little lie.

Moose thought about that for a minute and then asked, "How fath doeth it go?"

"One hundred knots, same as the Cherokee," I replied nervously.

"Whath good ith thath? I can outrun a Cherokee in my hog in third gear."

"Right. I guess they'll never catch you, Moose."

His scarred face split into a big toothless grin. "Yeah."

A week or so later, Henry mentioned that Moose was ready to fly his first solo that afternoon.

"When he comes back, I'll distract him and you hit him with the bucket of water."

"No way," I said. "You throw it. Nobody needs to distract Moose. He's permanently distracted."

"I'm going to tell him you said that."

"And I'll tell him that you don't like flying with him and that's why you refused to throw the water."

Our childish exchange continued to a draw. Neither of us

was willing to throw water on a six-and-a-half foot, 300-pound beer disposal.

"You're chicken," Henry said.

"You're right," I replied.

I tried to arrange my lessons to be in the air when Moose went on his first solo in case someone did splash him but it didn't work out. I was in the lounge when Moose ducked through the door toothless but grinning like a little kid. It was obvious that he had been sent on his own.

Henry shook his hand with a wince and made a ceremony of presenting him with a First Solo Certificate. There was no water in sight. I didn't volunteer any.

Moose filled in his log book and put his "X" on the invoice for the flight. Henry had another student waiting but Moose didn't leave right away. He was enjoying the recognition and looking around expectantly.

"I thoughth thomebody wath thupoed to throw wather on me," he said.

The lounge went silent. Henry looked at me. I looked back and shrugged my shoulders. Nobody was looking at Angel. She slid off her stool and hoisted a full-sized garbage can onto her shoulder. It was half-filled with water and must have weighed 100 pounds. Moose was leaning against the counter with his back to her. Angel climbed onto the rungs of her stool for height and tipped the can toward Moose. He didn't see it coming and her aim was perfect. The contents landed on his head and soaked him to the floor.

The man nearly drowned. I was ready to run out the front door. I could see that Henry was ready to follow. Moose shook off the cascade and came out laughing.

"Yeah, thath more like ith," he declared and gave Angel a big grin.

Later that day Henry asked Angel why she had broken her cardinal rule about water in the office.

"The man needed a bath," she said simply. "I wouldn't have missed it for the world."

151

Chapter Forty-two

Barnacle Bill

I watched as a ski-equipped Aeronca Champ, cocked in one almighty sideslip, came out of nowhere and slid down to the snow-covered infield in front of the Derry Air flying school. It was early on a calm Saturday morning in December. I was standing in front of the window of the lounge waiting for my first student and hoping the coffee would connect my brain to the rest of my body before he arrived.

I had never seen the Champ before. As it taxied over the lumpy, snow-covered grass toward the office, I could see the details of an original Aeronca paint scheme, mostly cream coloured with a big red teardrop on the bottom of the fuselage. The airplane stopped just short of the snow ridge on the edge of the ramp and shut down.

The arrival of a skiplane was an unusual event at Derry's medium-busy, controlled airport in slushy southern Ontario. I continued to watch as the Aeronca's door flopped forward against the wing strut. A short, stocky pilot hopped out. He was dressed in a black snowmobile suit, big laced boots and one of those winter police hats with ear flaps. He was carrying two short pieces of wood in a heavy pair of leather gauntlets. He bent under the right wing strut, used his shoulder to rock the airplane and slid one of the sticks under the right ski. He tramped around to the left side and repeated the procedure. When he was done, the pilot scrambled over the low snow bank and waddled across the ramp to the office. I smiled and nodded to him as he came through the door.

"She's nippy out there, eh?" he said with a friendly grin. His face was red and leathery. As he spoke, the direct telephone line

152

connecting the flying school to the control tower rang.

"Yup, I guess it is," I replied, walking over to the phone. "Hello?"

"Tower here," the voice on the other end of the line said. "I want to talk to the pilot of that rag wing airplane who just landed on the infield."

The man in question was stamping his feet on the entrance mat and removing his gloves.

"The tower controller wants to talk to you," I said, holding the phone out to the newcomer.

He ambled over to the desk, unzipping his bulky suit. "'ello?"

I could only hear the pilot's side of the conversation. It was interesting.

"O' course I landed with no clearance, I got no radio, eh," the newcomer said and then listened patiently for a minute.

"Well, there was no tower 'ere the last time, eh."

"Five years? That's what I thought, it's new, eh."

He listened again for a while.

"Well, why would I be putting a radio in an airplane that's got no electrics? It don't make sense, eh."

"Sure, whatever you say." He hung up.

He wrinkled his brow and looked at me. "He sounded a bit excited, eh."

"Didn't you talk to anyone on your way in?" I asked.

He gave me an odd look. "Well, I'd be talkin' to myself if I did. I got no one else with me, eh."

My student arrived, so I didn't have a chance to continue the conversation. I mentally named this character Barnacle Bill and went to work. During the pre-flight briefing with my student I noticed Barnacle Bill bought a coffee and wandered around the lounge reading the bulletin board and looking at the pictures. When I was signing out, he bid us a "goodbye" and headed for the infield. We followed him to our aircraft. While my student was doing a pre-flight inspection, I watched "Bill" pull the sticks out from under the Champ's skis and put them in the back of the airplane. He leaned into the cockpit and set the controls. Then he hand-propped the engine while standing behind the propeller. Two flips and it settled into a nice, easy idle. With the engine running, Barnacle Bill walked behind the tail, picked it up and turned the airplane into the wind.

153

Something caught my eye in the control tower. They were flashing him an intermittent white light, the no-radio signal for "Return to starting point." There was no other traffic.

Bill either didn't see the light or chose to ignore it. He climbed into the airplane, closed the door and applied full power. In a hop, skip and a jump, he was in the air.

The next Saturday morning I watched for Bill from the lounge window, my coffee in hand. He didn't disappoint me. The bright little Champ came curving toward the infield from over the hangar row. Barnacle Bill was good. He had the Champ sideways and dropping like a rock. I held my breath. At the last possible second, he snapped the airplane straight, checked the descent, raised the nose, and settled onto the snow in a perfect three-point landing. The Aeronca stopped beside the ramp across from Derry Air.

The tower telephone rang before he had cleared our door. It sounded like the same controller as the previous week and he was hot.

"Good morning," I said to Bill, "The tower wants to talk to you."

"Boy, she's a bit nippy out there, eh?" he said, stamping his feet. He walked over to the desk.

"'ello?"

"Well, I didn't call you 'cause I got no radio. I told you that last week, eh."

"It doesn't make sense to get a radio when I got no electrics, eh."

"Well, o' course I started 'er by 'and last week, she's got no electrics. I told you that."

Barnacle Bill was frowning and shuffling his feet, but I think he was showing more patience than the controller.

"Well, how would I be starting 'er with someone in the front seat if I'm the pilot, eh?"

"Okay, whatever you say."

He looked up at me. "I hate to say it, but the boys in that tower are a little t'ick in the 'ead, eh?" he said. "He told me not to do whatever he says I'm doing, again."

I had a few minutes before my first student, so I drank my coffee with Barnacle Bill. I found out his name was Roy Barlett and he was from "up country a piece". He had spent the last 10-odd years rebuilding the Aeronca after flipping it over in soft snow.

"I redid the engine, while I was at it."

I tried to gently suggest that the control tower was there to separate the traffic so that made it necessary for aircraft using the airport to get prior permission before flying in the control zone.

Roy leaned over to look out the window. At that time on a Saturday morning, there were no airplanes moving for 50 kilometres.

"'e's got his work cut out for 'im, eh," Roy said with a grin.

I couldn't help thinking that this shorter version of Grizzly Adams was living a forgotten but important era of aviation. Hopping to a nearby airport for coffee on a sunny Saturday morning in an old, slow airplane should be what pleasure flying was all about. From across the ramp, Roy's airplane looked to be in good shape and he flew it well. The regulations that he was breaking were designed for a different kind of flying, the orderly commercially-based aviation necessary to handle large volumes of high-speed traffic. This early in the morning, he wasn't bothering anyone. I couldn't help thinking that perhaps Roy's style of aviation was more fun.

My student arrived and Roy left. I saw him hand prop the engine, turn the tail, climb in and takeoff while the tower flashed its white light.

The next Saturday he was back. This time, when the airplane stopped on the other side of the snow bank, Roy left the engine running while he put the sticks under the skis and walked to the office. The tower phone was ringing when he was halfway across the ramp.

"Good morning, it's for you," I said when he came in the door.

"Thank you," he replied. "It's a bit nippy out there, eh."

"You can say that again," I replied.

"'ello?"

"O' course I left 'er runnin'. Last week, you give me the devil for 'and proppin' 'er, eh."

"Well, she's got no electrics, eh. A starter wouldn't be doin' me much good, now would it?"

"My licence number? I don't have a pilot licence. My dad taught me how to fly. He didn't have one either."

"The airplane registration? She doesn't have one. I just rebuilt 'er after the crash, eh."

"Whatever you say."

He hung up and looked at me. "He said he's sending someone over. I don't know what for. I got nothin' to show 'em, eh."

He scratched his head for a moment. "I think I'll take my coffee to go."

He did.

As he was turning the airplane around by the tail, the tower telephone rang. I could see they were flashing their red light at the Aeronca this time.

"Hello?"

"Tower here. We can't see any registration on that airplane. Can you?"

"No, I can't see any registration, either," I said. It was the truth.

The little airplane accelerated across the infield.

"Who was the pilot?" the controller asked.

"His name? It's Barnacle Bill."

The next Saturday, "Bill" went somewhere else for coffee. Wherever that was, I hoped to find it some day.

Chapter Forty-three

Beautiful Bob

There is nothing in the Flight Instructor's Manual about how to handle amorous students. Flying lessons become a close relationship between the teacher and pupil. The two are partners in the student's dream of learning how to fly. They share the miscues and triumphs of each lesson. Training cockpits are small. Regular shoulder rubbing and the odd touch are part of each lesson. This has led to the occasional flying school romance. It happened to Henry.

Henry was a natural flying instructor. He liked people, loved to fly and made his students feel that they were important.

Enter Bob. Bob was a lonely, older optometrist who was of the male-to-male persuasion. His latest live-in friend had left him. Bob turned to flying lessons to meet new people. He found Derry Air and was assigned to Henry.

Bob swished into the Derry Air lounge like a female model on the runway at a fashion show. He bent his wrists, rolled his eyes and gave a little squeal whenever he was excited, which was often.

Word about Bob spread quickly through the flying school staff. When he was scheduled for his second lesson, the mechanics took a special coffee break just to see him.

Darcy immediately nicknamed him Tinkerbell. "He must be the fairy godmother," the chief mechanic said. "No wonder he wants to learn how to fly."

Eric, Henry and I were having coffee together later that day.

"What's it like flying with Bob?" Eric asked.

"Interesting," Henry replied.

"That's not good enough," Eric said. "Tell us more."

"Well, he's not a natural born pilot. He leans into me whenever we bank the airplane to the left, but I think it's just nervousness."

"He wants you Henry," I said, trying to stir things up. "He can't help it."

"Yeah, well, he can't have me."

On their third lesson, Bob gave Henry a present. I wasn't there, but Henry told me about it.

"I had mentioned that my sunglasses were loose. During our pre-flight briefing, Bob gave me a pair of top-of-the-line Aviators. I didn't think too much of it. He is an optometrist. I figured that he got them free or cheap. I thanked him, he squealed a little and we went flying. In the air, he continued to lean against me in left turns. This time he was reluctant to straighten up when the turns were finished. I asked him to stay on his side of the cockpit. He apologized and said he didn't realize that he was doing it. I hope this doesn't get worse."

"What will you do if it does?"

"Take a holiday and book him with you."

"Thanks for the warning. I'll start making heterosexual jokes so he won't want to fly with me."

Despite the fact that Bob didn't fit the macho image of a pilot, he became well liked at Derry Air. He went out of his way to be friendly to everyone and it worked. We were getting used to having him around when he sashayed in for a lesson on Valentine's Day and presented Henry with a small gift-wrapped box. In hindsight, Henry should have given it back unopened, but he had been caught off guard. He opened it. It was a silver Rolex.

"I noticed that you didn't have one of those aviator's watches," Bob explained with a little squeal.

"I can't accept this," Henry said.

Bob's delight turned to a pout. "It's just a token to show you how much I appreciate the lessons," Bob whimpered.

Henry looked like he wasn't sure what to do. We were all watching him, but no one was helping. He pocketed the watch. "Let's go flying."

Later, Henry had coffee with Eric and I.

"Thanks for nothing with Bob today," Henry said.

"If you don't like the Rolex, I'll take it," Eric offered.

Henry grinned for the first time that day, pushed the watch across the table and said, "It's yours, but you have to fly with Bob from now on."

Eric pushed the watch back. "No thanks."

"Well, we have to do something," Henry said.

"It's an opportunity, Henry," I said with a laugh. "Give in to it. The man is old and rich. Lie back and enjoy it. You could be set for life."

"No thanks."

"I'll make you a deal," Eric said. "Talk to him once more. Tell him that Derry Air is flying lessons only: no presents and no crossing over the flap handle in the cockpit. If that doesn't work, then I'll tell him he'll have to fly somewhere else."

That cheered up Henry. "I didn't think Irv would let us kick someone off the course."

"He wouldn't, but I'm betting it won't come to that. If it does, let me worry about it."

"It's a deal."

Henry's talk seemed to work on Bob. He was still friendly to everyone but there were no more presents. Whenever I asked Henry how it was going with Bob, he said, "Fine."

That might have been the end of the story, except Henry experienced a stuck microphone the day he sent Bob on his first solo flight. They flew a couple of circuits together and then Henry called for a full stop landing. He had Bob pull off onto a taxiway and then radioed to the control tower that the student was going to fly his first solo and the instructor was going to walk in from beside the runway. He hung up the microphone but the transmitter stayed on.

I was in the office. Everyone could hear Henry explaining to Bob that he was going to send him on his first solo. Bob squealed.

"Kiss me good luck," we heard Bob say.

"No, no kissing. You go flying and you'll be fine. Just do everything that I told you."

There was the sound of rummaging. I thought it was Henry undoing his seat belt but apparently it was Bob digging in his flight bag.

"Then kiss my Teddy good luck," Bob said, "or I won't go. This is very emotional for me."

There was a small smooching sound and then Henry could be heard opening his door. "One circuit and I'll see you back in the lounge," Henry said, "Have a good one."

"Ohhhh," Bob whined.

There was a long silence followed by the sound of Bob picking up the microphone. "Derry Tower, Tango Victor Hotel is ready for takeoff."

The use of the microphone unstuck the transmitter relay.

"Tango Victor Hotel is cleared for takeoff Runway 06," the controller said. "The wind is zero six zero at five to ten."

"Tango Victor Hotel."

Henry walked into the lounge. I could have kept my mouth shut, but I didn't. It was more fun not to. Besides, I decided that word would get around through one of the staff or customers who had heard the soon-to-be-well-known "Kiss my Teddy" exchange.

I went up to the flight desk where Henry was signing the student First Solo Certificate that Angel had prepared. He looked at me. I closed my eyes, puckered my lips and said, "Kiss me."

At first he was surprised. "What are you talking about?" he exclaimed.

"The microphone in TVH stuck open," I replied. "Congratulations, you're famous."

"The whole conversation?" he moaned.

"Every Teddy little bit," I said.

By then, Bob had landed and was clearing the runway.

"Congratulations on your first solo," the controller said.

"Thank you very much," Bob replied.

"You and Teddy did a good job," the controller continued.

"Why thank you," Bob said with a little squeal. "You know Teddy? Who is this?"

"Tango Victor Hotel is cleared to the ramp via Charlie and Foxtrot."

Henry looked deflated. I blew him a kiss.

Chapter Forty-four

Circus

Henry suffered a lot of ribbing after the "Kiss-my-Teddy" first solo flight. Whenever Darcy, the world's most sarcastic aircraft mechanic, saw Henry, he would pucker his lips and say, "Kiss me or I'll die."

Henry would tell him to get lost, "You're not my type," he'd say.

Bob never came back to Derry Air. Henry called him several times but Bob made different excuses for not booking a lesson.

He was dead two months later. The cause was not disclosed but he must have known that his time was limited. The first solo must have been a personal, final goal.

Henry went to the funeral. A few weeks later he received a letter from a lawyer. It said that Henry had been named as one of Bob's beneficiaries. A cheque for $55,000 was enclosed.

Henry didn't mention the money at work. He told Susan and me when we were having dinner at his house one evening in February with he and Leanne.

"That's great, Henry," I said. "I told you the old guy would be worth it. What are you going to do with the money?" I assumed he was going to say something like, "Pay off the mortgage".

"I want to start my own flying school," he said.

I was caught off guard. Henry and I had talked about how much we liked instructing but as far as I knew, we were still headed for the airlines. Henry and I were good buddies. My support for the idea probably meant a lot. I surprised us all.

"What about me?" I blurted out.

Henry, Leanne and Susan stared at me. It was Susan, who was used to my wandering mind, who recovered first.

"I think Henry was looking for a different reaction," she said.

"Well, I thought that Henry and I were joining the airlines together," I said. "If he's going somewhere else, then I'm not so sure about me."

"I thought you were the one sold on the airlines," Henry countered. "Your resolve had me convinced. It wasn't until the money from Bob came along, that I seriously considered anything else."

"It was you who convinced me," I said. "I followed you to Derry Air for the multi-engine instrument flying experience that would lead both of us to the airlines."

"Well, Leanne and I have talked about it a lot. There's room for another flying school in the town of Circus. The population is close to Derry's. The only school is part of a sleepy flying club. I've watched Mingy make easy money long enough. I figure a small operation at Circus could do well. What do you think?"

"What do I know about running a flying school?" I said. "I'm not going to be the one to push you into it."

"Well, I was hoping you'd do more than that," Henry said. "I need a partner. I want my own flying school but I can't work seven days a week and also raise a family. I thought you might join me."

I looked at Susan.

Henry spoke again. "I know you two will have to talk about it. This is not something we should rush, but if we are going to do it this year, it should be in the spring."

Susan jumped right in. She must have been reading the "Yes" look on my face.

"Have you done any planning for it, Henry?" she asked.

"Funny you should ask," Henry said with a smile. He disappeared into their den and came out with a file.

The four of us spent the rest of the evening talking about how Henry and I might establish a flying school at Circus.

"There are no facilities to rent at the local airport," Henry said. "We'd have to start from scratch on leased land. It's going to be costly to finance buildings and aircraft. Setting up for aircraft maintenance will also be expensive. There will have to be money for promotion. The cost of getting started is another reason for having a partner."

We talked on. It grew late. We decided that Henry would make discreet inquiries at the Circus Airport. Susan and I said we'd talk about the partnership and get back to him. Before we left, Henry proposed a toast to Bob.

"To Bob," I said.

"Who was Bob?" Susan asked.

"A friend," Henry said. "A student who became a friend."

Chapter Forty-five

The Flying Circus

On the way home from Henry and Leanne's that night Susan was supportive of the flying school partnership idea. It was a big sacrifice. I would be trading a steady income for the chance of no income and a guarantee of a large debt. We discussed a second mortgage on the farm so we could be equal partners with Henry. Susan taught riding on Sundays outside in the cold. I was sure that an indoor riding arena was on her mind, but it went unmentioned.

"I'm making good money," she said, "and we're young. If we're ever going to do something like this, it should be now. Start your flying school."

"Thank you." It was all I could think of to say.

"You're welcome. Now it's two o'clock in the morning and I'm going to bed."

She gave me a kiss. "Good night sky pilot."

"Good night. I love you."

I turned the lights out and sat at the kitchen table in the dark. Lady slept at my feet. I thought about the fun of running a flying school with Henry. The airport at Circus was smaller than Derry's. There were no scheduled airline flights. It would be more of a grassroots flying school. The rush of the idea blocked out the financial risk. I could only think positively. After a while, I couldn't think of not forming a partnership with Henry.

At 03:00 a.m., I phoned him. He was still awake. "Hello," he said as calmly as if it was the middle of the day.

"Hi," I said quietly. "It's a go."

"Good. I knew you would."

"I'll see if I can arrange a second mortgage on the farm," I said, "so we can do it 50/50."

"Great."

"See you at work."

"Good night."

The second mortgage was so easy it was scary. I filled in an application. I thought the bank manager would want a pile of paperwork including financial projections for the new business.

"No," he said focusing on Susan's salary. "Your wife is making enough money to cover it. Get her to co-sign and the money is yours when you are ready," he said.

I told Henry that the money had been arranged and that he had a partner for better or worse.

We shook hands on it. "One hurdle down and a million more to go," he said, but he was smiling.

Our biggest fear in launching the flying school was losing our jobs before we were ready to start. A premature loss of income would be a tough setback. The day after Henry visited the manager at the Circus Airport, Mingy called the two of us into his office. He closed the door.

"What are you calling your new flying school?" he asked straight out.

I was shocked.

Henry was ready. He looked Mingy square in the eye. "The Flying Circus," he said.

"I like it," Mingy said. "I'll lease you two Cherokees to help you get started."

"Why would you do that?" I blurted out. "We were trying to keep it a secret so you wouldn't fire us."

Mingy ignored me and looked at Henry. "He's a good instructor," he said, nodding his head in my direction, "but he has a lot to learn about business."

Then he turned to me. "I'm going to lease you two airplanes because they are old and tired and I need to get rid of them. This way they make me money. I don't fire you because I don't have replacement instructors yet. I've arranged with Eric for you to work here until you get an operating certificate for your school and we get more staff. Angel will help you with the government paperwork. When you start, the airplanes come here for maintenance. It'll keep my shop busy. I've already arranged it with Darcy. Any questions?"

I couldn't speak. Miserable Mingy had just solved our one million hurdles.

"No, sir," Henry said. He stood up and shook his hand. "Thank you very much."

"Welcome to long hours, high stress and hard work. Now get out of here, get back to work and take this glider pilot with you."

"Yes, sir!"

About the Author

Garth Wallace is from St. Catharines, Ontario. From 1971 until 1990, he worked at various locations as a flying instructor, bush pilot and corporate pilot. It was this period that inspired his four books of funny flying stories. Wallace now lives near Ottawa with his wife and works as a publisher for the Canadian Owners and Pilots Association.

Enjoy other books by Garth Wallace:

Fly Yellow Side Up

This is the humorous story of a suburban pilot who moves north seeking the freedom and glory of flying float planes. It is the ideal situation for a city slicker to make a fool of himself. You won't be disappointed.

Pie In The Sky

Ride with Wallace at a small-town flying school where he discovers cowboy ag-pilots, Mennonite buggy buzzing and other off-the-wall aviation adventures.

Blue Collar Pilots

This is a lighthearted tribute to the real pilots in aviation, the low-profile cockpit grunts who don't fly aircraft that fly themselves: bush pilots, ag flyers, courier dogs, water bombers, instructors, fighter jocks, cargo haulers and helicopter pilots.

Don't Call Me a Legend

Charlie Vaughn is Canada's most famous modern day general aviation pilot. *Don't Call Me a Legend* is the exciting story of how Vaughn became a world-renowned pilot. It is a legacy of modern aviation stories that are unique to anything that has ever been told.

All of Wallace's books are available from:
Happy Landings
RR # 4
Merrickville, Ontario, Canada
K0G 1N0

Tel.: 613-269-2552
E-mail: orders@happylanding.com

or at better book stores and pilot supply shops.